Hi . . .

I'm D____ S___ _nd I'm trying to find my Star
_____ _ecial
_____akes me _____ out from the crowd.
I'm not exactly sure what that will be, but
our class are putting on a fashion show at school.
I can't help thinking that might be a sign.

Maybe I am cut out for a life in the spotlight?
I am pretty sure I have what it takes.

Sadly, I also have a goat, three chickens, a crazy
dad, a heartbroken sister and a whole raftful of
worries . . . not what you need when you are
chasing dreams of catwalk stardom, trust me.

I'm in trouble – big trouble. And wriggling out
of this one might be tricky . . .

Hugs, happiness and custard doughnuts . . .

Daizy Star
(aged 11)

*Books for younger readers*

SHINE ON, DAIZY STAR

DAIZY STAR AND THE PINK GUITAR

STRIKE A POSE, DAIZY STAR

*Books for older readers*

DIZZY

DRIFTWOOD

THE CHOCOLATE BOX GIRLS: CHERRY CRUSH

DREAMS AND DOODLES DAYBOOK

LETTERS TO CATHY

# cathy cassidy

Strike a Pose, Daizy Star

PUFFIN

PUFFIN BOOKS

Published by the Penguin Group

Penguin Books Ltd, 80 Strand, London WC2R 0RL, England

Penguin Group (USA) Inc., 375 Hudson Street, New York, New York 10014, USA

Penguin Group (Canada), 90 Eglinton Avenue East, Suite 700, Toronto, Ontario, Canada M4P 2Y3

(a division of Pearson Penguin Canada Inc.)

Penguin Ireland, 25 St Stephen's Green, Dublin 2, Ireland (a division of Penguin Books Ltd)

Penguin Group (Australia), 250 Camberwell Road, Camberwell, Victoria 3124, Australia

(a division of Pearson Australia Group Pty Ltd)

Penguin Books India Pvt Ltd, 11 Community Centre, Panchsheel Park, New Delhi – 110 017, India

Penguin Group (NZ), 67 Apollo Drive, Rosedale, Auckland 0632, New Zealand

(a division of Pearson New Zealand Ltd)

Penguin Books (South Africa) (Pty) Ltd, 24 Sturdee Avenue, Rosebank, Johannesburg 2196, South Africa

Penguin Books Ltd, Registered Offices: 80 Strand, London WC2R 0RL, England

puffinbooks.com

First published 2011
002

Text and illustrations copyright © Cathy Cassidy, 2011
All rights reserved

The moral right of the author/illustrator has been asserted

Set in Baskerville MT Standard 13/20 pt
Printed in Great Britain by Clays Ltd, St Ives plc

British Library Cataloguing in Publication Data
A CIP catalogue record for this book is available from the British Library

ISBN: 978-0-141-33597-1

www.greenpenguin.co.uk

MIX
Paper from
responsible sources
FSC® C018179

Penguin Books is committed to a sustainable future for our business, our readers and our planet. This book is made from Forest Stewardship Council™ certified paper.

ALWAYS LEARNING                    PEARSON

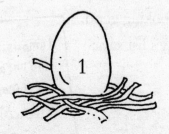

1

We are lolling about on the sofa, watching my little sister Pixie's DVD of *The Little Mermaid* for the 379th time and sipping hot chocolate with marshmallows on top. Pixie is spellbound. She knows every scene, every word, off by heart. It is her favourite DVD of all time.

For me, *The Little Mermaid* is more background noise. I am busy making a list of possible Star Qualities. My teacher, Miss Moon, is very keen on everyone finding their Star Quality, which is fine if you are great at singing like my friend Willow or brilliant at dance like my friend Beth, or even really arty like my best boy-mate Murphy Malone. It is not so good if you are me.

I cannot decide what my Star Quality should be.

I change my mind about every five minutes, and unless I can settle on one thing the chances of me getting Miss Moon's ultra-cool Star of the Week prize are not looking good.

So far, today's list says:

> famous actress
> mountaineer
> ice-cream taster
> Prime Minister
> ?

I am not sure if I am brave enough to be an actress, and there aren't very many mountains in Brightford, but I have had some practice at ice-cream tasting and I think I could be good at that. As for running the country, how hard can it be?

If I was Prime Minister, the first thing I would do is supply unlimited custard doughnuts for all schoolchildren, and then ban homework. Although some people actually like it – my big sister Becca, for example.

Becca is a kind of geek-Goth, with backcombed hair and black eyeliner and a green-fringed boyfriend called Spike who is not nearly as scary as he looks. Right now, Becca is curled up in an armchair, ploughing through endless pages of advanced algebra while listening to clashy-trashy music on her iPod.

She is very weird indeed, but not as weird as my dad, of course.

He is having some kind of a mid-life crisis and keeps on getting these terrible ideas that threaten to turn life as we know it upside down. Dad packed his job in a few months back to follow his dreams – which are actually like other people's nightmares – so he is usually around when we get home from school. If we are really unlucky, he will even have a special treat for us, like prune flapjacks or beetroot stew.

Tonight we should be safe, though, because it is Wednesday and that is the night Mum brings home fish and chips once she finishes her shift at the hospital. It is the best night of the week.

Today, when we got in from school, there was no Dad at all. There was just a note saying he would be back soon, which is why Pixie made straight for the

3

DVDs and I made straight for the hot chocolate, and Becca . . . well, Becca made straight for her iPod and her homework, but there is no accounting for taste.

The DVD is just finishing when Mum comes in, shrugging off her coat and scarf. She sets down the fish and chips.

'Hello, Daizy, hello, Pixie, hello, Becca . . .' she says, and then her eyes narrow and her voice starts to rise. 'GET THAT WRETCHED GOAT OFF THE SOFA!' she yells. 'I've told you a million times!'

Hmmm. I forgot to mention Buttercup. She is my pet goat, and a very annoying boy at school called Ethan Miller gave her to me for Christmas. Sort of.

It's a long story.

Anyhow, it seemed all wrong to make a baby goat sleep in the shed, especially in the middle of winter, so Buttercup sleeps in a dog basket under the kitchen table and sometimes, when Mum and Dad are not about, she sneaks into the living room and snuggles up on the sofa.

I push her off and she skitters across the carpet, one of the fluffy cushions clamped between her jaws. Little bits of fluff and chewed-up cushion trail

4

after her, evidence of another domestic disaster.

'Daizy!' Mum wails. 'Another cushion ruined! That goat has got to go!'

'Nooooo!' Pixie, Becca and I protest. 'Please Mum . . . no!'

'Well, she can stay in the shed then,' Mum relents. 'She's a goat, not a cat or a dog! Goats chew things! Your dad's running shorts, Pixie's slippers, Becca's school tie . . .'

'I like it better like this,' Becca shrugs, flicking out the tail end of her tie and examining the frayed bits.

Pixie ushers Buttercup out into the garden and Becca jumps up and puts the kettle on and starts setting the table and I take the fish and chips and start unwrapping them, and peace is restored. Almost.

'Where is your dad, anyway?' Mum huffs, sitting down at the table and squeezing ketchup on to her chips. 'He promised me faithfully he would keep an eye on that goat!'

'He left a note,' Becca shrugs. 'It said he has important business, and he'll be back soon.'

There's a crunching of gravel on the drive outside, and the slamming of a car door. Moments later, Dad walks past the window carrying several planks on his shoulder. Mum drops her fork with a clatter.

'Whatever now?' she groans.

We run to the door, Buttercup at our heels. Dad is unloading rolls of chicken wire from the roof rack of the car, whistling happily, and that has to be a bad sign.

'Mike,' Mum says firmly. 'What are you doing with all that?'

'Ah,' Dad says brightly. 'I'm building an ark!'

My heart sinks. An ark? We have been here before, back when Dad had his crazy plan to sail round the world. I thought he'd got over all that, I really did.

'An ark?' Pixie asks. 'Like Noah?'

'Did someone forecast rain?' Becca smirks.

Mum just folds her arms and glares at Dad and he holds his hands up, laughing.

'Relax!' he laughs. 'Not that kind of ark! I'm talking about an animal shelter. I'm going to convert the shed, for Buttercup . . . and build a run round it for the chickens!'

There is an ominous silence.

'What chickens?' Mum asks at last.

Dad opens the car boot and we all crowd round. Inside is a wire crate with three big, golden-brown chickens inside, squawking loudly and fluffing up their feathers.

'Oh, Mike,' Mum says weakly. 'What have you done now?'

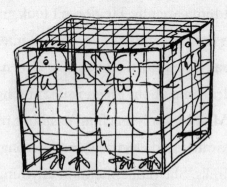

2

'Fresh eggs,' Dad says brightly. 'Think of it, Livvi. Healthy, organic, free-range . . . fried, boiled, poached, scrambled . . . our very own eggs!'

'Like on a farm,' Pixie chips in, and I have a sudden, alarming vision of Dad as a farmer in a flat cap and wellies, chewing on a bit of straw and carrying a pitchfork. It's not a good image.

'I've always wanted to go green,' Dad says.

I look at him carefully. He doesn't look green at all . . . he is the same mixture of pasty white and pink as usual. Then the penny drops. Green . . .

We are learning about green issues at school this term. Miss Moon is teaching us about recycling, and saving water, and electricity, and getting energy from windmills. She didn't mention anything about chickens and goats.

'It's time we stopped destroying the planet,' Dad says. 'I'd like us all to try out a simpler lifestyle, be self-sufficient, be more in tune with nature. We've always dreamt of this!'

'Actually,' Becca says, looking at Mum for support, '*We* haven't!'

Mum sighs. 'Those dreams were a long time ago, Mike,' she says. 'Besides, three chickens are not going to save the world! Fresh eggs would be very nice, but I don't suppose it is as easy as all that.'

Dad laughs. 'How hard can it be?' he shrugs. 'We could grow our own vegetables, collect our own eggs, have our own livestock –'

'Mike!' Mum says. 'No! You promised me you would consult the family before you launch into any more crazy plans. We cannot have livestock! We live in a semi-detached house in the middle of a town!'

'Well,' Dad says, looking slightly shifty. 'At the moment, we do . . .'

Becca chokes on a chip.

'I am NOT going to live on a farm!' she says icily.

Dad laughs. 'Of course not,' he says. 'And don't

worry, I have learnt my lesson. I won't be doing anything drastic unless you all agree. The chickens are just an experiment. I have been thinking for a while that I'd like to do some gardening, get some veggies on the go . . .'

Mum frowns. 'Well,' she says, 'I suppose it would keep you out of trouble until you find a new job.'

'Exactly,' Dad grins. 'It'd be a hobby. Well . . . for now, at least.'

'What does that mean, *for now at least?*' my big sister asks. 'That maybe, next week, you will change your mind and buy a tractor and a whole, entire dairy herd?'

'Oh, Becca,' Dad sighs. 'That's hardly likely, is it?'

I bite my lip. I have learnt just lately that anything is possible where Dad is concerned.

On the way to school I wonder how best to explain Dad's latest plan to my friends. Will they think that keeping chickens and goats in the back garden is weird?

It's not even as though we have an especially big house. If we had one of the big Victorian places in

Stella Street, it might be different. Just a few doors along from the school, there's this huge house set back from the road, all covered in ivy. It's kind of spooky, with big gardens, knee-deep in weeds – Buttercup and the chickens would have a field day in there.

'My dad brought home three chickens last night,' I mention casually, as Miss Moon collects our spelling-test books.

'Curried, or Kentucky Fried?' Willow grins.

'LIVE chickens, Willow,' I say. 'To give us fresh eggs.'

'Or fresh chicken nuggets,' Willow teases.

'Don't, Willow!' Beth wails. 'Those poor chickens!'

'They're free-range,' I reassure her. 'And I won't let Dad turn them into nuggets, I promise!'

Beth just sighs and shakes her head. It's not like her to get so gloomy over three small hens, but she hasn't been herself just lately. I expect she is still pining over Ethan Miller – having a crush on the most annoying boy in the school cannot be much fun. She and Willow have been crazy about him for months.

'Watch it, Daizy,' Willow grins. 'Your dad might swap the car for a combine harvester. Soon you will be wearing wellies and dungarees to school.'

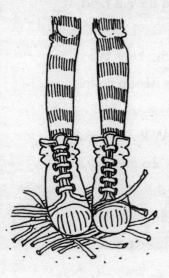

'No way!' I protest. I look down at my red Converses. They are probably not the right sort of footwear for mucking out a goat shed, but dungarees and wellies? No. I am not a country girl. The countryside is full of cowpats and muck spreaders and dung heaps, and raging bulls that might charge at you for no reason at all.

Miss Moon interrupts my thoughts with a brisk clap of her hands, and the class is silent.

'Today,' she says, 'as part of our project on Green Issues, we are going to talk about recycling. Can anyone tell me what recycling is?'

'A load of rubbish,' Ethan snorts, and his friends fall about laughing.

Miss Moon sighs. 'You are right, Ethan,' she says.

'Recycling is all about rubbish . . . and how we can turn it into something new. Well done.'

Ethan looks startled at getting the right answer, even if it was by mistake. His cheeks glow pink with pride. Seriously, he is a very annoying boy.

'So,' Miss Moon presses on. 'What kind of things can be recycled?'

A forest of hands shoot up into the air.

'Tins and bottles!' Murphy Malone says.

'Paper!' Willow adds.

'Cardboard!'

Miss Moon smiles. 'You've got the idea,' she says. 'Almost anything can be recycled.'

'I've seen recycled toilet roll in the supermarket,' Ethan smirks. 'Does that mean it's been used once already? Because that is kind of gross.'

A howl of disgust ripples round the classroom, but Miss Moon nips it in the bud. 'No, Ethan, it does not,' she says briskly. 'Recycled toilet roll is made from old newspaper and exercise books and scrap paper. Not from pre-used toilet paper, as you very well know.'

Ethan's shoulders droop a little.

13

'Glass, tins and paper can all be processed and turned into new, recycled glass or tin or paper,' Miss Moon is explaining. 'Even cabbage leaves and potato peelings can be saved and turned into soil to grow fresh vegetables.'

I groan. Dad has already explained that we will be saving our kitchen scraps from now on to feed to the chickens, and we already take all our tins, bottles and paper to the recycling centre.

'Lots of us already recycle,' Miss Moon is saying. 'That means less rubbish in our dustbins . . . but what about the stuff that's left? Empty packets and bubble wrap and silver foil and plastic bottle tops . . . is there a way of recycling any of that? Turning it into something useful or beautiful?'

Murphy Malone puts a hand up uncertainly.

'I expect you could make them into *something*, if you really tried.'

'Exactly,' Miss Moon agrees. 'How about clothes and accessories?'

Hands start shooting up around me, but my mind remains stubbornly blank. A load of old rubbish is just a load of old rubbish, surely?

'A party dress made from bubble wrap,' Willow suggests.

'Jewellery!' Sheena McMaster chips in. 'You could string the bottle tops together to make bracelets and necklaces and dangly earrings.'

'Skinny jeans made from sweet wrappers,' Murphy Malone offers. 'Worn with a binbag T-shirt!'

I look around. The class are grinning, buzzing, full of ideas. Only Beth looks as doubtful as me. Bubble-wrap party dresses? Bottle-top earrings? Sweet-wrapper jeans? I don't think so. Who wants to look like they're wearing the contents of their own rubbish bin?

'Wonderful!' Miss Moon says. 'And a perfect starting point for our project! You are going to design and create a whole fashion collection made from recycled materials, and put on a show for Year

Five. I want you to see just what can be achieved when you start thinking green!'

A fashion show? I blink, my imagination sparked at last.

'This is all about turning rubbish into something beautiful, useful, cool,' Miss Moon says. 'It will take imagination. It will take creativity and vision!'

Hmm. Maybe there is something in this. Miss Moon makes it sound kind of cool . . . perhaps it could be fun.

Dustbin fashion, here I come!

3

Murphy goes on about his ideas for the recycled fashion project all the way home. He has so many ideas there are bound to be some to spare, which is good, because I am not sure that dustbin fashion is going to be my Star Quality. Besides, I am kind of preoccupied with the chickens and whether they have laid enough eggs yet to bake some cupcakes for after tea.

So I am not really paying attention as I walk along Silver Street with Murphy and Pixie.

And then, suddenly, the smell hits us. A putrid stench rises up from nowhere and has us coughing and gagging.

'*What is that?*' Murphy chokes. 'They must be working on the drains!'

'Or the sewers,' I groan, wrinkling my nose.

'Smells like a farmyard,' Pixie says.

A feeling of dread settles in the pit of my stomach. A farmyard. Surely this can't have anything to do with Dad . . .?

We reach the gate of number seventeen and I forget about the stink for a whole split second. My front garden looks like a bomb has hit it. Dad is standing in the middle of what was once the lawn, digging trenches and shovelling dark, stinky soil around.

'Nooooo!' I wail. 'What have you done? Does Mum know about this?'

'Not yet,' Dad beams. 'But I know she'll be impressed!'

I seriously doubt that. Horrified is more the word that springs to mind.

'Um . . . what about the grass?' Murphy asks. 'And the flower beds?'

'Oh, that won't matter,' Dad assures us. 'Grass and flowers are just for decoration. Potatoes are a *crop*!'

He reaches into a sack made from orange nylon netting and holds up a shrivelled, scabby-looking potato with pale beansprouty shoots all over it. 'See?'

It is not a pretty sight. Pixie takes a step back. 'Urghhh!' she shrieks. 'It's disgusting! And what's that awful stink, anyway?'

'My farmer friend has delivered a trailerload of well-rotted manure,' Dad explains. 'To make the potatoes grow faster!'

'It smells like *poo*,' Pixie says.

'It *is* poo,' I tell her, through gritted teeth. 'That's what manure is. Farm-animal poo.'

'Exactly, Daizy,' Dad says. 'We'll make a farmer of you yet!'

'Er, no, thank you,' I say politely.

'Those potatoes look yucky,' Pixie frowns. 'I'm not eating them. Not after they've been in the ground. With the poo.'

'Now, now, Pixie,' Dad grins. 'Of course you will eat the potatoes, when they are ready. That's where potatoes grow – in the ground! And these lovely seed potatoes haven't been sprayed with nasty chemicals, either. They're organic!'

Pixie's lower lip trembles.

'I don't like potatoes any more,' she whimpers. 'I'm going to show Murphy the chickens.'

Dad sighs. 'No problem, Pixie,' he says. 'I've made them a beautiful chicken run to live in. I think they're going to like living here. They will be laying eggs soon!'

No eggs yet then. No cupcakes for after tea.

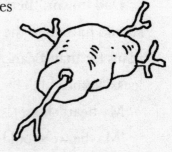

Pixie leads Murphy through to the back garden, while Dad examines the shrivelled potato a little sadly.

'Will she really refuse to eat them, do you think?' he frowns.

'Probably not,' I say. 'It won't be these spuds, anyway, will it? These are just the seeds. Don't worry about it, Dad.'

'I am a bit anxious,' he admits. 'Bert from next door looked over the fence and asked what I was doing earlier. He said that nobody plants spuds in February.'

Bert next door is an expert gardener who wins prizes for his roses and keeps half the neighbourhood supplied with carrots and onions from his allotment.

'I might be a little bit early with my crop, but that's why I am adding lots of manure,' Dad explains.

'It's going to look a bit of a mess, isn't it?' I sigh.

Dad frowns. 'Bert said that,' he admits. 'Perhaps I should have used the back garden, Daizy, but I have plans for that. Beans, turnips, courgettes, carrots, leeks, lettuce . . .'

My heart sinks.

'Maybe we should tidy it up a bit before Mum gets back?'

'Maybe,' Dad agrees. He chucks in the last few spuds, buries them in manure and rakes the soil, but it still looks as though a small bulldozer has gone crazy in there.

As for the manure heap, it's as high as the window sill, and it really, really pongs.

Dad doesn't seem to notice.

'There,' he says, looking around proudly. 'That's much better! Wait till your mother sees all this!'

I blink. I think I might try making myself scarce before then.

A bloodcurdling scream comes from the back

garden. 'Da-aad!' Pixie screeches. 'Dai-zeee! Help!'

Oh dear.

We run through to the back garden, with its newly customized goatshed and chicken-wire enclosure. Inside it, Buttercup the goat is grazing peacefully. She looks up, all sweet and innocent, as if she would never even think of chewing a school tie or a pair of running shorts.

Pixie's eyes are brimming with tears.

'It's the chickens!' she blurts out. 'They've gone!'

Murphy frowns, peering into the shed. 'I think there might be one left in there.'

'They're all in there,' Dad says confidently. 'They'll be lying low, just getting used to it. They can't possibly have escaped, because I built this run myself and it's totally, one hundred per cent escape-proof . . .'

At that exact moment, a little, brown hen emerges from the shed, squeezes through a small gap beneath the wire and sprints for the bottom of the garden.

We watch, stunned, as she flaps up on to the fence, looks around briefly, clucking, and vanishes from sight on the other side.

A rabble of barking starts up somewhere nearby and Pixie's eyes grow round with terror.

'We'd better try and catch them,' I tell Murphy. 'Before it gets dark.'

'I had names for them and everything!' Pixie wails. 'Cleopatra and Esmerelda and Attila!'

'Wasn't Attila some kind of crazy tyrant from history?' Murphy asks. 'He went around terrorizing people. Attila the Hun.'

'Attila the Hen,' Pixie says, a tear rolling down her cheek. 'She was my favourite.'

I raise an eyebrow. 'They all look the same, Pixie,' I tell her gently. 'You haven't really had time to decide on a favourite.'

'She was the brown one,' Pixie insists. 'With the really pointy beak.'

We cannot find the chickens anywhere. We look under the shed, in the garage, in next-door's garden and right along the street, peering under every single car. Where could they have gone?

We search on until after dark, when Murphy goes in for his tea and Mum arrives home. Guess what? She is not impressed.

'Mike!' Mum says, through gritted teeth. 'I have had a seriously stressful day. I was looking forward to relaxing with my family, not chasing about the streets hunting for lost chickens. And as for the front garden . . . you agreed not to do anything drastic without asking us first!'

Dad looks a little guilty. 'I just wanted to make a start on being self-sufficient!'

'You *promised*, Mike,' Mum says. 'This was just a hobby, you said! The place looks like a bomb site!'

'I can fix the garden!' Dad argues. 'And the girls will find the chickens. I really want this to work – we had such big dreams, once. Living in the country, living close to nature! Give this project a chance, Livvi, please!'

'One chance,' Mum agrees. 'You've got a couple of weeks, Mike, to show me this can work – and if it doesn't, we forget about it. Deal?'

'Deal,' Dad says. 'I promise!'

We have a makeshift supper of toast and jam and

go to bed early, but it feels like my head has barely hit the pillow before I am wide awake again. The thin, dawn light is filtering through the curtains, and Pixie is jumping up and down on my bed, laughing.

'They're home! The hens are home!' she says. 'Look!'

I crawl to the window, lift the curtain and peer down into the garden. Three brown hens are sitting neatly on top of the shed, huddled together in the dawn chill.

As we watch, the biggest hen – Attila – stands up, stretches and struts a little before unleashing a bloodcurdling early-morning alarm crow.

*Cock-a-doooodle-doooo!*

I grit my teeth. Great . . . a hen that thinks it's a cockerel. Mum is just going to love that . . .

4

In class, the Great Green Fashion Show is taking shape. A mountain of rubbish appears in the library corner, the raw materials for our designs. There is cardboard, newspaper, bubble wrap, scrunched-up wrapping paper, tin foil, sweet wrappers, crisp packets, bottle tops and shiny CDs – a treasure trove of junk.

Perhaps this project could be a chance for me to find my Star Quality at last? I could be a fashion designer! I sneak a look across the table to where Murphy is sketching out ideas in the middle of his spelling-test book. It's an arty, elegant design . . . the kind of thing you might see on the catwalk, worn by one of those very cool boy-models.

My dreams fizzle and die. Who am I kidding?

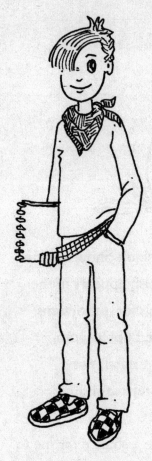

Murphy Malone is the
designer here. With his
dipping fringe, studded
belt and chequerboard
Vans, he is just too cool
for school.

This project is made
for him. After years of
bending the school
uniform rules, he finally
has a free rein to be as
wild and wacky as he likes.

In case you are
wondering, that is
pretty wild and wacky.

When Murphy starts
rummaging through the waste paper and junk and
sketching out cool, crazy ideas, other kids begin
to do the same. The classroom is buzzing – and
things are looking good.

Only Beth is stuck for ideas. She is still very
quiet and listless, which is a little bit worrying.
I think of my theory that she is pining for

Ethan Miller, but I can't help wondering if something else is wrong.

'Are you OK, Beth?' I ask. 'You seem a bit down this week.'

'Not really,' she sighs. 'I can't think of anything for this project. And things are just . . .' I wait for her to say more, but instead she frowns, and I see a glimmer of tears in her bright blue eyes. 'Oh, look, it's nothing, Daizy,' she says. 'Just me being silly. I'll tell you about it another time, right?'

She turns to the rubbish pile and picks up a handful of shredded office paper. I'm about to ask her again when Murphy comes over and interrupts us.

'Hey, Beth,' he says. 'You do ballet, don't you? You should design a tutu!'

'Maybe . . .'

'Use the shredded paper for the skirt!' he suggests. 'With some of this old crumpled tissue paper underneath. That would look cool!'

Beth holds a froth of crumpled tissue and shredded paper against her waist. She twirls a little and the flicker of a smile appears.

'Thanks, Murphy,' she says.

'Your tutu is going to be brilliant,' I say encouragingly.

Me, I am aiming for a kind of urban farmgirl look. I have made a top from orange nylon potato netting, weaving in chicken feathers, goat hair, potato peelings and bits of chewed-up old cushions for texture and variety. I will add a skirt created from brown-paper goat-feed sacks, and wear a garland of garlic on my hair like a tiara.

'Interesting,' Miss Moon says when she sees my design.

Urban farmgirl

She can't say any more, of course, but I can't help thinking it might just put me in the running for the Star of the Week award.

But after Friday, when Sheena McMaster gets the Star of the Week award for making earrings and a

necklace from ring pulls,
polystyrene and
scrunched-up sweet wrapper
foil, I decide that maybe
designing is not my Star Quality.
All the same, making fashion

out of a load of old rubbish is risky, daring –
you would need someone confident, stylish and
elegant to wear it. Someone young and quirky,
cool and cutting edge.

Someone like me!

My Star Quality is staring me in the face – I could
be a model! I have experience – I have been wearing
clothes all my life. And after all, how hard can it be?

Willow reads a lot of teen mags . . . she might
know more.

'Willow,' I say during class on Friday afternoon.
'How do models get discovered? Do you have to go
to college or something, or can anyone learn?'

'I don't think you go to college,' she frowns.
'I think that anyone can be discovered and shoot to
stardom. There are these people called model scouts,
and their job is to look out for young people with

potential. Models can get spotted anywhere. At the hairdresser, in Topshop, in the street . . . it's kind of random.'

'Really?'

'Really,' Willow nods. 'Model scouts can be anywhere. They spot you and they sign you up for their model agency, and the next thing you know you're flying to Paris to appear on the cover of *Vogue*!'

'Wow,' I breathe.

My heart starts beating faster. My Star Quality is much more dramatic than fashion design – it's something that will put me centre stage, that will put my name in lights.

I am going to be the world's first pre-teen supermodel.

How cool is that?

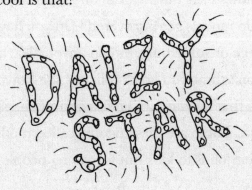

5

I don't suppose there are many pre-teen
supermodels who have to live on a farm,
though – even if it is a small, garden-sized one.
I expect that most supermodels live in exotic
places like Paris or New York, and they probably
do not have to share a space with an eccentric
dad, an exhausted mum, a Goth big sister and
a little sister who thinks she is a mermaid. And
that's not mentioning the goat or the three badly
behaved hens, obviously.

Still, I am doing my best.

I have read every fashion mag I can get my hands
on and tried to find out all about famous models like
Lily Cole and Kate Moss.

And now Becca is showing me how to get the

catwalk strut, which involves wiggling your bottom and taking very long strides wearing a pair of Mum's high-heeled party shoes. Seriously, it is harder than it looks.

'I'm not sure about this,' I say, but Becca waves my protests away.

'Models have to wear high shoes,' she insists. 'It gives them a long, lean outline that shows the clothes off to best advantage. Models have to be tall, Daizy, and let's face it, without the shoes you are just a titch.'

I ignore the pain and the sudden fear of heights and shake off Becca's arm. I wiggle my bum and tilt my chin up towards the ceiling, which means I cannot see very much at all. It probably looks quite elegant, though.

I manage three shaky steps across the bedroom floor before I trip on the edge of the bedspread and crash into the dressing table, ending up in a heap on the floor with the bedclothes tangled round me. Mum and Dad run upstairs to see what the racket is.

'I'm practising to be a pre-teen supermodel,'

I say, by way of explanation. 'But I might start
without the shoes. Sorry!'

'It's OK, Daizy,' Mum sighs. 'I thought it was that
wretched goat again!'

I am not too pleased at being mistaken for a goat,
but I decide to let it pass. Mum's not too pleased,
either, not after what happened earlier this week . . .

Twice lately, Buttercup has managed to chew
through the fence and make a break for it. Only
yesterday, we found her upstairs in Becca's bedroom,

eating a maths text book. I think it gave her indigestion.

The trouble is that when Buttercup escapes, the chickens follow, and those chickens have a talent for trouble.

Three days ago Margie Brown from next door opened up her shopping basket in the middle of Tesco and found Attila the Hen inside, nesting peacefully among the paper tissues and old shopping lists. Mrs Brown screamed and Attila flapped out and made off down the aisle, squawking loudly and terrorizing the customers.

Dad had to go along to rescue Attila, who was flapping about in the aisle that sells frozen chicken.

I think she was probably staging some kind of protest.

The *Brightford News* was full of the story that evening. *Tesco Chicken Rises From Dead in Frozen Food Aisle!* the headline shrieked, and there

BRIGHTFORD
NEWS
60p
TESCO CHICKEN
RISES FROM DEAD
IN FROZEN FOOD
AISLE!

was a photograph of Attila fluttering about next to a freezer full of chicken drumsticks.

'If I'd known she was asleep in my shopping bag, I'd never have taken it,' Mrs Brown explained. 'I got such a shock . . . but I wish I hadn't screamed!'

'It's not your fault, Margie,' Mum said later on the phone. 'I don't blame you for screaming. I'd have done the same. It won't happen again. If it does, those chickens are history!'

I bite my lip at the memory.

The trouble is, I have got quite attached to Buttercup and the chickens – I don't want Mum to give them away now. Who would want them, anyhow? No farmer would touch them with a bargepole . . . no egg farmer, at any rate. There are other kinds of farmer, of course. The kind who supply the frozen chicken aisle in Tesco, for example . . . it doesn't bear thinking about.

So I decide not to say anything about the goat comment. Instead, I tidy up the bedroom carnage, put Mum's party shoes away and slip outside for a quiet chat with the chickens. Within seconds, I spot Buttercup trying to unlatch the gate of the enclosure with her teeth. I can tell that she is missing the days when she had the freedom of the house. I expect she is pining for a mouthful of fluffy cushion or one of Dad's slippers to chew. I let myself into the run and bat her gently away from the gate.

'Listen,' I whisper urgently. 'Things are getting serious. You have to stop escaping, all of you. No more eating Becca's maths books. No more nipping down to Tesco. You have enough to eat, you have a warm shed and a big run . . . you need to stop escaping!'

Buttercup blinks and bites a chunk out of my school skirt. 'No!' I sigh, exasperated. 'You have to cooperate! Buttercup, you have to grow up a bit so you can start producing milk. And the rest of you . . . well, lay some eggs! Is that so difficult?'

The hens look up at me, baffled, as if I have asked them to start speaking French, and my heart sinks. Unless they stop escaping and produce some eggs, their days here are numbered. They are not pet material, and they're not farmyard material, either. If they don't change their ways pretty fast, they are more chicken-nugget material than anything else.

I can see I will have to take things into my own hands.

I check through my pockets and find a handful of loose change and a piece of string. I let myself out of the gate, tying the latch up with string behind me.

I have a plan.

6

I nip to Tesco and buy six free-range eggs. Back at the chicken run, I dust one of the eggs with soil, stick a feather to it with mud, then hide it just inside Buttercup's shed.

I think about hiding all six, so that I know the chickens are definitely safe, but I decide to take this slowly. I can hide another egg tomorrow, and more later in the week. Hopefully, by then, they'll be laying their own.

I wander back inside, trying to act naturally. Dad is at the cooker making a vat of nettle soup.

'Have you checked for eggs today?' I ask casually.

'Yes,' Dad says with a sigh. 'Nothing, I'm afraid.'

'They might have laid something now . . . you could check again.'

'I'll try tomorrow,' Dad shrugs.

I sigh. Patience has never been my strong point. 'Please, Dad,' I say. 'You never know. And I would really like a boiled egg!'

'I'm busy, Daizy,' Dad says. 'You go and have a look, if you like.'

'But I want *you* to go!' I beg. 'Please! I was so, so sure that today would be the day . . .'

Dad puts the lid on the soup pan. 'Well,' he says. 'I wanted to check on Buttercup, so perhaps I will take a little look while I'm out there.'

Two minutes later, Dad is back in the kitchen, yelping with glee, holding the egg aloft.

'You were right, Daizy!' he announces. 'They've done it! They've finally done it! There will be no stopping them now!'

I go a little bit pink, but nobody notices. Dad
hard-boils the egg and divides it up between the
five of us, along with some dandelion leaves he has
made into a salad.

'A celebration dinner!' he announces, as we sit
round the table. 'This is all our own produce!'

'Woop-de-doo,' Becca says, raising an eyebrow.

The thrill of keeping the chickens safe a little
longer begins to fade as I realize that the celebration
dinner is actually very, very small.

'There's not much of it,' Pixie comments, looking
at her plate in dismay.
'Is this it?'

'No, no, there's the nettle soup too!' Dad beams.

I am not sure a garden full of dandelions and nettles is much to be proud of, but Dad's potato crop has not shown any signs of life, and nor have the vegetables he planted in the back garden. The window sill is full of apple seedlings in little pots, because he is planning an orchard, but judging by the weedy seedlings it could be twenty years before they are ready to fruit. That is a very long time to wait for a pudding.

'I might go over to Kirsty's house after tea,' Pixie decides. 'They're having pizza, with chocolate pudding and ice cream.'

Mum puts down her fork and pushes her plate away.

'Mike,' she says, in the kind of tone you might use when talking to a very small child. 'One egg, divided between five people, and a heap of dandelion leaves . . . are you serious?'

'It's free-range!' Dad says proudly. 'From our very own hens! And the salad leaves are organic!'

'I'm putting some burgers in the microwave,' Mum says. 'OK?'

43

'What about the nettle soup?' Dad protests, but Mum puts the burgers in, gets rolls from the bread bin and roots in the cupboard until she finds Jaffa Cakes too.

'Egg salad is all very well,' Mum says. 'But we are not quite ready to be self-sufficient yet, Mike . . . not on one solitary egg and a handful of weeds. The children are growing. You can't expect them to survive on dandelion leaves and nettle soup.'

I think that some supermodels eat mainly soup and salad, but I have to admit that burgers and Jaffa Cakes are more my kind of thing.

'There will be more eggs soon,' Dad promises. 'And potatoes, beans, turnips, courgettes, carrots, leeks, lettuce . . . apples from our own trees . . . and goat's milk and cheese too, once Buttercup is a little bit older!'

'Goat's cheese?' Becca echoes, going a funny shade of green.

'No,' Mum interrupts. 'This little farming project has been very . . . erm . . . interesting, but I think we have to accept that keeping hens and a goat in the middle of a town is not working out.

Admit it, Mike – this particular dream is over.'

'Well . . .'

'It's over, Mike,' Mum says firmly. 'Promise me! Tearing up the garden for non-existent potatoes, chickens flapping about in the supermarket and frightening the customers. This has gone far enough!'

'OK, Livvi,' Dad says solemnly. 'Fair enough. I'll sort it, I promise.'

Just then, the lights flicker and go out, leaving us huddled in the dark.

'Power cut?' Dad wonders out loud. 'Fuse?'

Becca finds a torch and we shine it into the living room. In the yellow spotlight, we can see that the room has been ransacked, as if by a gang of vandals. Books, bags and cushions have been strewn across the carpet, cups have been overturned and the waste-paper basket has been emptied and chewed until it looks more like a mangled straw hat.

In the middle of it all, Buttercup is lounging across the sofa, munching on the table lamp. She has already gnawed right through the electric

45

cord and looks up, a picture of innocence, as she
delicately crunches the lampshade.

Oops.

7

It has been Beth's turn to hold a sleepover for a while now, but nothing has been said.

'It's ages since we've had a proper get-together outside of school,' I hint, as we work on our fashion creations in class one afternoon. 'Shall we do something this weekend?'

Beth looks up from her shredded-paper tutu, which is starting to look pretty cool. 'It's my turn, but I'm not allowed a sleepover at my place just at the moment,' she says. 'Dad says he's got too much on his plate already.'

'What kind of things has he got on his plate?' I frown.

If he is anything like my dad, it will be stewed dandelions and raw beetroot, but I'm not sure this is quite what Beth means. I think she means that her dad is worrying about something.

'Oh, just stuff,' Beth says vaguely. 'You know.'

I actually do not know, but I don't suppose it can be all that serious or Beth would tell us about it. Wouldn't she?

'Come to my place instead,' I say. 'I can show you the chickens, and we can practise for the fashion show and try out hair and make-up ideas.'

'I am not wearing any make-up,' Murphy Malone growls. 'And I don't think any of the other boys will, either.'

'Boys are so dull,' I shrug. 'You never want to try anything new.'

This is not strictly fair, as the boys in Year Six are looking less dull by the minute, and it is mainly down to Murphy Malone. He has got the whole class fired up for this fashion show – even Ethan Miller, who is making an armoured vest by slicing up old fizzy-drink cans, flattening the foil and linking the bits together with wire. I think he is only interested because he gets to wear protective gloves and use tin snips, but still, with Murphy's help, the

Coke-can vest might just work out.

Willow looks up from her bubble-wrap ballgown. 'A sleepover sounds cool,' she says. 'Count me in.'

'Me too,' Murphy shrugs. 'I won't stay over – I don't want to spoil your girlie fun – but I'll come for a while. And I'll bring custard doughnuts.'

'OK,' I grin. 'Beth?'

'Um . . . I'm not sure,' she says quietly. 'I am not really in the mood for a sleepover . . . and I'm not exactly mad about this fashion show, either.'

'But you have to be!' I say, alarmed. 'You have never missed a sleepover before. It wouldn't be the same without you! And the fashion show will be awesome! I have some really cool ideas!'

Beth sighs. 'OK, Daizy,' she says, 'I'll be there.'

On Saturday night, the sleepover is in full swing. We have cuddled the chickens, taken Buttercup for a walk in the park, eaten custard doughnuts and talked non-stop about the fashion show. Well, I have talked non-stop about it, anyway.

Now we are all dressed up in our fashion-show costumes, which is slightly bizarre, but also quite cool, and I am showing Beth, Willow and Murphy my best catwalk wiggle.

'I am not doing that,' Murphy says. 'No way.'

'You have to,' I tell him. 'It's what models do!'

I have already painted stripes of purple eyeshadow across his cheeks, warpaint-style, and gelled his hair into a towering quiff copied from one of Willow's teen mags, but Murphy has had enough.

'Don't get carried away, Daizy,' he says. 'It's not like a real fashion show!'

'It could be!' I say. 'We could get the papers along, and invite a few of those talent scouts from the model agencies that Willow was telling me about. Maybe they could put it on the local TV news! We could all be famous!'

I pause for breath, quite pleased with my little speech, but I am not sure the others are convinced.

There is a silence, and then Beth laughs, a harsh, mocking sound.

'I don't think so,' she snaps. 'It's just a stupid school project, Daizy. Nobody's going to put it on the news, and nobody's going to be famous.'

A dark blush begins to seep across my cheeks, and my heart thumps. I open my mouth to argue, but nothing at all comes out. Beth is one of my best friends in the whole world, and she just made me feel as rubbish as the junk we have been making our costumes from.

Beth seems to be feeling pretty rubbish too, because she tears off the shredded-paper skirt she has been wearing over her jeans, and storms off to the bathroom, locking herself in.

'What did I say?' I whisper, shell-shocked.

'Nothing, Daizy,' Willow sighs. 'Nothing bad, anyway. You were just going on a bit about the fashion show, and . . . well, I don't think Beth is that into it.'

'But it's exciting!' I protest. 'One of us could get spotted by a model scout and end up on the cover of *Vogue*, right? Just like you said!'

'It's not very likely,' Murphy says.

'It might be,' I argue. 'I have been practising for weeks now. I have been studying my sister's fashion mags and researching on the Internet, and I am pretty sure I've got what it takes.'

'What it takes to do what?' Willow asks, puzzled.

'To be the world's first pre-teen supermodel,' I explain.

'Is this about finding your Star Quality?' Murphy wants to know.

'It might be,' I huff. 'It's all right for you, Murphy. Everyone knows that you are going to be a fashion designer one day. And Willow will be a pop singer with a string of hit albums, and Beth will be a prima ballerina . . . but I will still be looking for my Star Quality when I am old and grey, unless I do something now! The fashion show could be my big break!'

'Er . . . maybe,' Murphy says.

This isn't quite the response I was hoping for, but then Willow puts an arm round my shoulder. 'Of course it could,' she says kindly.

'I'd better go and talk to Beth,' I say.

'Are you in there?' I call, knocking gently on the bathroom door. 'We're going to watch a film before Murphy goes home. OK?'

The door opens slightly, and Beth emerges, her eyes a little red and damp-looking. 'Have you been crying?' I ask, alarmed.

'No! I just had something in my eye!'

'Look, I'm sorry I was going on a bit about the fashion show,' I say. 'I didn't mean to get on your nerves.'

'It's not you,' Beth sighs. 'It's me. I've got a few things on my mind, that's all. I didn't mean to be so grumpy!'

'It's just that I was hoping that modelling might be my Star Quality,' I explain.

'Why not?' Beth shrugs, and hope unfurls inside me again.

Then I remember what she said about having things on her mind, and I frown. 'Beth, is something worrying you? Is something wrong? Do you want to talk about it?'

'No, no,' she says, brushing my concerns aside. 'I'm fine. Let's watch the film, OK?'

We go back through to the bedroom and snuggle down to watch the movie, and it's only much later, after Murphy has gone home and the rest of us are sleeping, that I know for sure that Beth is not fine. In the darkness, I'm almost certain I can hear her crying, curled up under a borrowed duvet.

But when I ask her what's wrong, she just rolls over and pretends to be asleep.

8

I try to ask about the crying the next day, but Beth tells me I was imagining it and makes me promise not to say anything to the others.

'I'm OK,' is all she will say, but I know that Beth is not OK at all. I just don't know what to do about it.

It's after school on Monday, and I am trying to take my mind off all of this by practising my supermodel walk. Becca and Pixie are making me walk up and down the living room with a big pile of books balanced on my head, and trust me, it is not easy. They are library books Dad has borrowed to brush up on potato farming and chicken keeping, and they weigh a ton, and I am wearing recycled platform shoes I have made myself from old cardboard and garden twine. They are not easy to stand up in, let alone walk.

'Come on, Daizy,' Becca sighs. 'Stand up straight! You need to move with elegance and grace!'

'I can't move at all!' I protest, as the books crash down to the carpet. 'It's impossible!'

'Try again,' Pixie says. 'I thought you wanted to be the first pre-teen supermodel?'

Two hours and lots of falling over later, we are finally making progress. Becca has resorted to hitting my shoulders with a rolled-up newspaper if I slouch and Pixie is dangling a custard doughnut under my nose. She says I can eat it once I manage a whole ten steps without dropping a book. There is nothing like the promise of a custard doughnut to focus the mind.

I try to forget that half a library is perched on my head and step out bravely. One step. Two. Three, four, five . . . and suddenly I know I can do it, and I am strutting my stuff, my head held high and just the tiniest hint of a wiggle in my walk. The books stay put at last, like a very heavy and slightly unlikely hat.

I make it to the other side of the room and Becca cheers as I lunge for the doughnut and allow the books to clatter down at my feet. I can do it! I really can!

'*Finally,*' Pixie sighs.

'I'm a natural, right?' I grin.

'Er . . . probably,' Becca says. 'I mean . . . definitely. Maybe.'

I dip down to collect up the fallen library books, my mouth full of sugar, and then I blink and my mouth goes dry, in spite of the custard doughnut.

One book, *The Complete Home Farmer*, has fallen open on a page I really, really wish I had not seen – a page about how to kill a chicken. There are

diagrams on how to wring the chicken's neck, then pluck it and take out its insides ready for the oven.

There is even a recipe for chicken pie.

Becca is helping me pick up the books, and she sees it too. 'Look,' I hiss. 'Dad wouldn't do that . . . would he?'

'Nah,' Becca whispers. 'It's just what farmers do when their chickens aren't laying any eggs . . .'

'What do they do?' Pixie asks brightly.

'Nothing!' I say, snapping the book shut.

Pixie's eyes narrow. 'Tell me,' she says. 'Tell me the truth. What do farmers do?'

I swallow hard.

'The thing is, Pixie . . . well, farmers have chickens for two reasons.' I feel like the meanest big sister in the world, like I am about to tell her that mermaids don't exist. Not that she'd believe me, of course.

'Some chickens are for laying eggs . . .' Becca says carefully.

'That's right!' Pixie agrees. 'And what are the others for? Is it something to do with feathers?'

'No,' I sigh. 'You know when we have roast chicken on a Sunday? Or chicken nuggets and chips? Or chicken soup?'

Pixie's eyebrows slide into a frown. 'Ye-es?'

'Well,' I tell her, 'that's the other thing chickens are farmed for. We eat them.'

I guess I should have seen it coming. Pixie

dissolves into tears, sobbing hysterically, and grabs the book from behind my back. It falls open at the gruesome chicken-pie page.

'Why didn't you tell me?' Pixie wails. 'Why didn't you tell me that chicken was made out of chickens? It's not fair! No, no, no, NOOOO!'

'Look,' Becca says. 'It's OK, because our chickens are laying eggs! One the other day, one yesterday, and two this morning! Stop worrying, both of you!'

I bite my lip. 'Actually, they haven't,' I confess. 'I've been putting the eggs there. I bought them from Tesco.'

Becca rolls her eyes. 'Oh dear. Those chickens really are useless. Still, that doesn't mean Dad would ever turn them into chicken pie. You know that, don't you?'

Becca wipes Pixie's eyes and calms her down again. 'Trust me,' she tells us. 'He wouldn't. Look, let's go get a hot chocolate.'

We pile through to the kitchen, where Dad is standing at the cooker looking smiley as he stirs a big pan of soup.

'Hey,' Becca says brightly, mixing up three hot

60

chocolates. 'Something smells good, Dad! I bet that's not nettle soup!'

Dad grins. 'No,' he says. 'It's chicken!'

But before I can say anything, Pixie unleashes a blood-curdling scream.

'MURDERER!' she yells. 'Chicken-killer!'

Dad looks horrified. He stands and watches, speechless, as Pixie sprints out of the back door, sobbing, and Becca and I run after her. We peer into the chicken run. Luckily, for once, all three hens are present and correct. Pixie is hugging them each in turn, telling them we will protect them.

Dad follows us out, looking baffled.

'All I did was make chicken soup!' he sighs. 'It used to be your favourite.'

'Pixie thought you'd used one of our hens,' Becca says. 'Honestly, leaving that awful book around where she could see it . . . you know she has a very vivid imagination!'

'I have a vivid imagination too,' I say. 'That book is horrible!'

'Dad, I am not eating chicken any more,' Pixie says. 'It's cruel!'

'I second that,' I say.

Becca rolls her eyes. 'You'd better take chicken off the menu from now on, Dad,' she sighs. 'This is an official protest. Right?'

'Right,' Pixie and I chime in.

'I wasn't planning to make our chickens into a pie,' Dad argues. 'They are young! They have years of egg laying ahead of them. But a farmer has to know about these things. Sometimes, when a hen gets old and stops producing eggs –'

'No!' I protest. 'Whatever you are going to say . . . just, no!'

Dad's shoulders slump. 'Right,' he says, eyeing the

chickens with regret. 'Well, that's OK. I can always specialize in goat's cheese instead then. Or potatoes, because chips are practically the British national dish and there will always be a demand for spuds! It could even be nettles . . . nettle soup is very underrated.'

'Trust me,' I say. 'It really isn't.'

It is so typical that the one crop my dad can actually grow is a weed. I have visions of the back and front gardens filled with towering nettles, and Dad inside the house making vatloads of nettle soup ready to be tinned and labelled and stacked on supermarket shelves around the country.

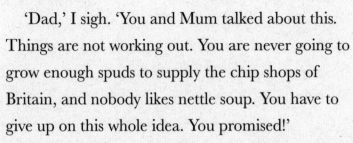

I don't think it will ever catch on.

'Dad,' I sigh. 'You and Mum talked about this. Things are not working out. You are never going to grow enough spuds to supply the chip shops of Britain, and nobody likes nettle soup. You have to give up on this whole idea. You promised!'

'Give up?' Dad asks, as if the thought has never

occurred to him. 'No . . . I didn't promise that. I said I would find a way to make it work. And don't worry, I have!'

My heart sinks. What now?

9

It is seventeen days now since the chickens arrived, and Dad calls a family meeting. I'm immediately suspicious – he has splashed out on takeaway pizza and ice cream and red wine.

'You're taking this very well,' Mum tells him. 'The end of the whole chicken-and-potato-farming experiment, I mean.'

'The end?' Dad laughs. 'It's not the end! This is just the beginning!'

'Mike,' Mum says sternly. 'You promised me!'

'I promised I would find a solution,' Dad corrects her. 'Keeping chickens and a goat in the town hasn't really worked out. So the logical thing seems to be . . .'

I pull a face. My dad is not at all logical, and

I dread to think what he might be planning next. I bite into a slice of pizza.

'Move to the country!' Dad announces.

I choke on my Deep-crust Mozzarella and Pineapple Surprise.

'No way!' Pixie, Becca and I chorus. Mum says nothing, but trust me, she is not looking happy.

'Hear me out, girls,' Dad barges on. 'Green fields, blue skies, fresh air! A little cottage with roses round the door! It was always our dream!'

'That was a very long time ago,' Mum replies. 'Besides, Mike, dreams are just that – dreams. In the real world, somebody has to earn the money to pay our mortgage – and that person is me, because you don't have a job any more, remember?'

'I do have a job,' Dad says. 'I am a farmer. On a small scale, obviously, but once we have our own smallholding . . . well, just think! I've been doing some research. Looking at remote smallholdings with several acres of land. I've drawn up a shortlist. Take a look!'

I wait for Mum to tell Dad not to be so ridiculous, but she just sighs, exasperated, and I watch my

supermodel dreams crumble into dust. I have
nothing against the countryside, I just do not want to
live there. And I definitely don't want to live in some
ramshackle farmhouse with nothing but fields for
miles around, while Dad tends his herds of goats
and chickens and raises endless crops of nettles.

Dad takes out a folder filled with papers, and my
heart sinks.

The first set of details show a derelict farmhouse
with no roof, in the south of Ireland.

'We'd get wet,' Pixie points out. 'And cold!'

An old barn in Cornwall and a rusting caravan
on the shores of Loch Ness get the thumbs down
too, as does an ugly bungalow in Wales and a tin
shed with a broken doorway on the Yorkshire Moors.
'They looked better on the Internet,' Dad says. 'I
mean, they do have potential, but –'

'But nothing,' Mum says. 'This is crazy, Mike.
Yes, I used to like the idea of living in the country
once . . . but even you must see that this is a joke!'

'I've saved the best till last,' Dad argues. 'Just give
it a chance, that's all I ask. We have to have vision!'

'You must have double vision if you think we

would be seen dead in these disgusting dumps,'
Becca snarls.

Becca has a point. I expect eyesight is one of the
first things to suffer when people get middle-aged. A
strong pair of glasses could be the answer. Dad looks
at the last few sheets, his eyes narrowing, which only
confirms my whole failing-eyesight theory.

He hands the papers to Mum, and she puts down
her glass of wine and studies the details carefully.

'Oh!' she says softly, raising one eyebrow. 'This
one doesn't look too bad. Perhaps I spoke too soon,
Mike. Maybe we should take a look after all?'

Dad slips an arm round her shoulders, and Mum
smiles. She looks at Dad, and she looks at the
property details, and her eyes are all faraway and
dreamy.

OK, now I really am scared.


Dad and Mum have fallen in love with a little
cottage on the Isle of Muck, way up on the west
coast of Scotland. I am not impressed. I mean . . .
Muck? Seriously? A name like that cannot be a
good omen, can it?

I have to admit that the island looks very pretty in the photographs, and that the cottage is beautiful, with whitewashed walls and red roses twining round the doorway.

Isle of Muck

I hate it on sight.

So what if it is pretty? So what if it has loads of land? So what if it is just two hundred metres from the beach? I don't care.

It is hundreds and hundreds of miles away from Brightford. This is where my friends are, and Beth and Willow and Murphy are the best friends ever. I will lose them, I know I will, if I go to live in the middle of nowhere.

I have seen it happen. I had a friend called Hasmita Patel, and when I was in Year Three, Hasmita moved away. We promised we would keep in touch and be friends forever, but after a while we just sort of stopped writing and phoning. I think that Hasmita forgot about me, and I forgot about her.

Perhaps Murphy, Beth and Willow will forget about me too?

As for finding my Star Quality, I may as well forget it. The Isle of Muck is no place for a supermodel, that much is clear.

There are some plus points to living on the Isle of Muck, I suppose.

Buttercup the goat might like it, because she will have fields to roam across and possibly some goat friends too. Cleopatra, Esmerelda and Attila can be as free-range as they like, and nobody will mind if Attila crows from dawn until dusk because, guess what, there are hardly any neighbours to complain.

I am not kidding. The whole island is just two miles long and one mile across, with less than forty inhabitants.

'It certainly looks idyllic,' Mum sighs. 'I don't see me picking up a senior nursing post out there, though!'

'Take a career break,' Dad says brightly. 'Recharge your batteries. Decide what you really want in life. You said yourself, Livvi, that job is wearing you down!'

'Yes, but –'

'I'm not saying you have to stop nursing,' Dad says. 'You could always go back to it. But . . . well, there are other things you've always wanted to do too. Grow herbs. Learn Spanish. Paint pictures, like you used to do. This is a once-in-a-lifetime opportunity! A little cottage with roses round the door . . . Liv, this place couldn't be more perfect!'

Mum shrugs. 'We could *look* at it,' she concedes. 'Just look, though, Mike! We would all need to be in agreement. And I'm not sure such a major lifestyle change would be a good idea, really.'

'It would be the best idea ever!' Dad grins. 'I'll make an appointment to view it right away! This cottage is available to rent, not to buy, so we could hang on to our house here until we were sure we'd made the right move.'

'Really?' Mum asks. 'We could rent this house out for a year, treat it as a trial, a chance to live the dream. And if things didn't work out . . .'

Mum not only seems to like Dad's crazy idea, she is actually joining in with his plans, which makes it seem a whole lot more real. And the thought of strangers living in our house while we are miles away on the Isle of Muck makes me feel sad and sick inside.

'Think of it!' Dad says. 'We wouldn't be needing a car any more . . . we could walk everywhere, or go by rowing boat. There's a ferry to the mainland three times a week, more in the summer. What a life!'

'Life?' Becca erupts. 'LIFE? You might as well bury us alive!'

Dad laughs. 'Honestly, Becca. You've been looking very pale lately . . . life in the country would do you good – give you nice, rosy cheeks!'

Becca is a fully-fledged Goth these days – I don't think she wants rosy cheeks, any more than she

wants wellies or a pitchfork or a straw hat.

'It would be a very green way of living,' Dad goes on. 'There is no mains electricity on the island – everything works on windpower! You'd approve of that, Daizy!'

'I would?'

It is one thing to be green when you live in a town – it just means recycling cans and bottles and turning down the central heating. Being green on the Isle of Muck might be very different. I picture the five of us huddled round a flickering candle, picking at congealed seaweed stew. I bet they don't have Topshop or New Look out there, either. What if I really do end up having to make my clothes out of feed sacks and potato netting?

'This is getting scary,' I whisper to my sisters, as Mum and Dad gaze, moon-eyed, at the cottage details.

'It is a bit,' Pixie says. 'I don't know if I want to live on an island called Muck. Although there could be mermaids . . .'

'Don't get your hopes up,' I sigh.

'They can't make us go,' Becca says darkly.

'Whatever happens, we all stick together on this. Agreed?'

'Agreed,' Pixie and I chorus.

That's something, I guess.

10

When I tell Beth, Willow and Murphy I might be moving to a remote Scottish island called Muck, they think I am joking.

'Your dad is losing it,' Willow sighs as we stand around in the playground waiting for the bell to go. 'I have never heard of the Isle of Muck! Are you sure he isn't just making it up?'

'I'm sure,' I say. 'It's real. I looked it up on the Internet. It's a tiny, windswept island off the west coast of Scotland, with more sheep and cows than human beings. Can you believe it?'

'All they need is a gang of chickens and goats to add to the population,' Murphy smirks. 'I wonder what you'd look like in a kilt?'

'This is serious!' I argue. 'Mum and Dad have

already fixed up a date to go and see the place. There is no escape! The fashion show is tomorrow, and I am on the brink of supermodel stardom, or a Star of the Week award at the very least. And now my whole life could be over!'

Willow and Murphy just laugh, but Beth looks suitably upset. 'I don't want you to go!' she says in a wobbly voice.

It is good to know that at least one of my friends will miss me.

'It might not happen,' I tell her. 'Apparently we all have to be in agreement, and I cannot see Becca agreeing to live on a tiny Scottish island, can you?'

'Not in a million years,' Murphy says.

'Your dad will never go through with it, anyhow,' Willow adds. 'A week or so from now, he'll have another crazy idea and forget he ever wanted to be a farmer. Trust me.'

Deep down, I know Willow and Murphy are right. Dad's brilliant ideas have a way of fizzling out like damp fireworks, so maybe all I need to do is stay calm and wait for the storm to blow over.

Then again, Mum has never been keen on

Dad's ideas before . . .

Beth doesn't look convinced, either. Her eyes are solemn and serious, as if she has her own personal raincloud hovering nearby.

Suddenly, a football crash-lands in my arms, just about knocking me over. Ethan Miller yells across the playground. 'Hey, chuck the ball back, Daizy! You can join in the game, if you like!'

I turn my back on him – Ethan Miller is a deeply annoying boy, and I do not want to encourage him. He likes to be the centre of attention. He will go to any lengths to ensure he makes an impression, even if it means trying to flatten someone with a football, or dropping a worm down their school sweatshirt (he did this to me in Year Three, and yes, I bear a grudge).

Besides, it was Ethan who gave me Buttercup, and Buttercup is what got Dad started on wanting to be self-sufficient. You could say Ethan is to blame for the mess I am in right now.

I hand the football to Beth. 'You chuck it back,'

I say. Beth and Willow both think that Ethan Miller is the best thing since custard doughnuts – they have been crushing on him all year, which is kind of icky to see, but if anything can cheer Beth up, it has to be Ethan.

'Nah,' Beth says. She lets the ball slide to the floor, allowing Willow to scoop it up and kick it over to Ethan.

I blink. Now I *know* there is definitely something very wrong – Beth is crazy about Ethan Miller. Never in a million years would she miss the chance to talk to him or chuck his football back.

'What is up with Beth?' I whisper to Willow. 'First there was the sleepover thing, and she's been so down in the dumps lately!'

'I don't know – she hasn't said anything to me. Maybe she's just stressed about the fashion show tomorrow – I don't think she's been looking forward to it,' Willow says. 'Hey, Ethan! Hang on! Murphy and I will play footy with you!'

Willow drags Murphy off into the scrum, and I turn back to Beth. Ever since the sleepover I've known things weren't right with her, but I've been

hoping it would just blow over, sort itself out. I've had enough problems of my own, but I can see now that's no excuse for ignoring a friend in need.

'Beth, I know something's bothering you,' I say. 'Tell me. Please?'

She shrugs. 'It's just . . . well, one minute everything is fine, just the way it has always been. The next minute . . . BAM. Everything changes. You never know just what is round the corner.'

'I know what you mean,' I say. 'Living with my dad has been a bit like that just lately. But, Beth – has something happened? Is something wrong?'

She sighs. 'It's nothing. I'm just feeling a bit gloomy today.'

'But you're OK?' I check. 'Really?'

'I can't talk about it right now,' Beth says, and her smile is a little too bright, as though it might dissolve at any moment. 'Thanks for caring, though, Daizy. I will tell you, I promise – soon. Don't say anything to Willow or Murphy, OK?'

'OK,' I say uneasily.

It turns out that Beth is right, though. You never know just what is round the corner, and this time it just happens to be Becca and her boyfriend Spike. I am walking home with Pixie and Murphy, and as we turn into Silver Street, there they are, in the middle of the pavement, talking very loudly and waving their arms about.

'Be reasonable!' Spike is saying, which makes me smile because my sister is many things, but reasonable is not one of them.

'I can't believe you won't help me!' Becca says, her voice rising to a howl. 'I can't believe you would abandon me now, in my hour of need! Drop me just

when I need you most! Cast me aside and trample
all over my heart with your size-nine biker boots!'

'Becca, listen . . .' Spike says, but my sister is way
beyond listening. Tears are streaming down her face,
making her black eyeliner run, and her voice is hurt
and harsh and angry, all at the same time.

'It's all over between you and me, Sebastian Pike,'
she yells. 'I never want to see you again. And you
know what? I won't have to. Because I will be

spending the rest of my life wasting away on some muddy rock out in the ocean hundreds and hundreds of miles from here. And it will all be YOUR FAULT!'

She runs off along the street, her crimped hair fluttering behind her in the breeze, and moments later we hear the front door of number seventeen close with an earth-shattering slam.

Spike looks slightly shell-shocked. He blinks and frowns and finally spots us glaring at him from the corner of the street. 'I can explain,' he says.

'Don't even bother,' I say loyally. 'Come on, Pixie. Murphy.'

I stick my chin in the air and march defiantly past, with Pixie and Murphy trailing along behind. I don't know what Spike has done, but it must have been pretty bad for Becca to dump him.

He may be a scary, six-foot Goth-guy with a green fringe and a pierced lip, but Becca loves him. At least . . . she did.

# 11

Becca locks herself in her bedroom, crying and playing her thrash-metal-punk CDs so loudly that everyone in the house feels like crying too.

It is not exactly a restful way to spend the evening before your big debut as a pre-teen supermodel, but I try not to be selfish. Becca's feelings come first, obviously.

'She was too young to have a boyfriend, anyway,' Dad is saying. 'It's all for the best. She'd be better off concentrating on her schoolwork. And now she won't have to worry about long-distance phone calls and visits when we go to live on the Isle of Muck.'

'*If* we go,' Mum corrects him. 'Besides, Becca is fourteen. She works very hard at school, and she has to have *some* fun.'

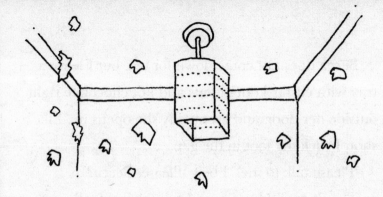

'Does that sound like fun?' Dad asks, as Becca ramps up the volume on her CD player so high that a few flakes of plaster drift down from the ceiling in protest.

'Spike seemed like such a nice boy,' Mum sighs.

'Teenage boys are all the same,' Dad frowns. 'I should know – I was one once. No, Becca is better off without him. Maybe now she will forget all this silly Goth nonsense.'

'Maybe,' Mum shrugs. 'I suppose you're right; perhaps it is all for the best.'

I can't quite believe my ears. Nobody seems to understand that my sister's heart is breaking . . . or remember that tomorrow is my big debut as a model. Mum and Dad are too wrapped up in their island dreams.

85

Becca does not come down for tea, but I leave a tray with custard doughnuts and hot chocolate right outside her door, and eventually she opens up. Like a shot, I stick my foot in the gap.

'Please talk to me!' I beg. 'Please, Becca?'

The door slides open and I sneak inside. Becca is curled up on her bed, hugging her ancient teddy bear.

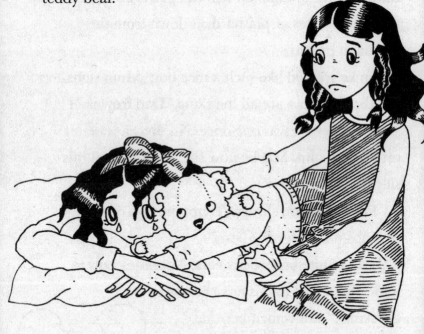

'I'm really sorry about Spike,' I say.

She sighs. 'Me too. He is SO not the boy I thought he was. I am better off without him.'

Becca starts crying again, her shoulders shaking, her eyes red and bloodshot. I pass her a box of tissues. 'Boys are bad news, Daizy,' she tells me, blowing her nose noisily. 'Don't ever get mixed up with them, seriously.'

'I won't,' I promise. 'I will be way too busy being a pre-teen supermodel, anyway. The fashion show is tomorrow, remember? I'm a bit nervous. You could help me practise my catwalk strut, if you like! It might take your mind off Spike.'

'You'll be fine,' Becca says listlessly. 'Just walk tall and keep your chin in the air. Oh, and, like I said – avoid boys. They will break your heart into a million little pieces and wreck your dreams and then laugh in your face.'

'Er . . . right . . .' I say. 'What exactly did Spike do?'

'I told him about the Isle of Muck,' my sister whispers. 'I told him that I had a plan.'

She starts to wail again. 'He . . . he . . . he refused to run away with me! I had it all planned! We were going to go to Paris and live on the streets and make a living busking on the banks of the River Seine!

87

Spike said it was a ridiculous idea and there was no way we could run away before our GCSEs, and that our families would be devastated. He doesn't love me, Daizy! He has ruined my life!'

I bite my lip.

'Let's get this straight,' I say. 'You dumped Spike because he refused to run away with you to live rough on the streets of Paris? You were going to run away and leave me and Pixie behind to wither away on the Isle of Muck, not knowing if you were dead or alive?'

'I'd have sent you a postcard,' Becca shrugs.

'Thanks a bunch,' I huff.

Becca rolls her eyes. 'Look, I couldn't have taken you two, could I?' she argues. 'There's no way Pixie could be expected to live in a cardboard box under the Eiffel Tower.'

'It's all right to expect her to live on a smallholding on the Isle of Muck, though,'

I growl. 'I thought we agreed we would all stick together on this?'

Becca's eyes brim with tears. 'We will be sticking together now,' she says. 'We'll be stuck on that stupid rock for the rest of our days, picking nettles and weaving our own kilts out of seaweed and heather.'

'That's not going to happen,' I say firmly.

Becca gives me a pitying look.

'Why fight it?' she snuffles. 'The way I feel right now, I don't care if I am stuck on a windswept island for the rest of my life. Let's face it, the further away I am from Spike, the better – I never want to see him again!'

'You don't mean that,' I argue, but judging by the look in her eye I think perhaps she does.

'Boys are nothing but trouble,' Becca declares tragically. 'Spike has broken my heart. Once we are on the Isle of Muck, I will devote myself to maths and science and violin practice. It's all I have left now.'

Well, at least Becca will have that.

Without my chance of supermodel stardom,

without my cool teacher or my three best friends,
I will have nothing at all. I bite my lip, and my whole
body feels shivery and cold.

If even Becca is resigned to life on an offshore
Scottish island, there is no hope left for me. No
hope at all.

## 12

Of course, once I get to school next day there is no time to worry about heartbroken sisters or mad chickens or my future as a goat farmer on the Isle of Muck.

It is fashion-show day, and I cannot stop myself from grinning with the excitement of it all, even if my life is in ruins. We are in the school hall getting ready. I twirl around in my potato-net-and-feed-sack frock, staggering slightly on my homemade cardboard platform shoes.

All around me, kids are laughing, chatting, making last-minute adjustments to their costumes. Girls are fluffing out the skirts of prom dresses made from scrunched-up Tesco bags and boys are pulling on jackets made from old copies of the *Beano*.

Willow's bubble-wrap ballgown looks like something out of a fairy tale.

A makeshift catwalk has been put together from staging blocks, Luka is testing out his sound system and Ali is fiddling with the spotlights he's borrowed from the school drama cupboard. Ethan Miller's cola-can vest makes a very pretty tinkling noise every time he moves. He hands me a roll of Sellotape and tries to get me to fix up a rip in his newspaper trousers, but I scowl at him and stomp away.

'OK?' I ask Beth, who looks stunning in her shredded-paper tutu. 'I know you're not crazy about this whole fashion-show thing, but . . .'

'I'll give it my best shot,' she promises, biting her lip.

'I know you will,' I grin. 'Oh, Beth . . . this is so cool!'

The place is a riot of colour and creativity, a tribute to the power of recycling. Ian Knox, who comes to school every day on a bike, has taken the whole recycling thing literally. His whole costume is made from old bicycle parts. His trousers are draped with punkish bicycle chains, his top is made from old

inner tubes and shredded
tyres and he is wearing
brightly coloured
wristbands made from
coiled brake leads.

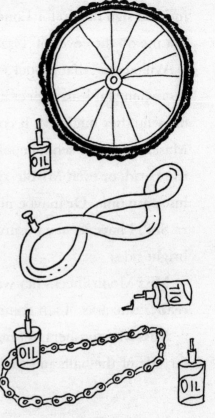

Somehow, he has
rigged up a dynamo light
on each shoulder, so that
he flickers slightly
whenever he moves,
and on his head he is
wearing a hat made
from a warped
bicycle wheel with
fluorescent armbands
woven in and out of
the spokes. Several small oil cans hang from the rim,
jangling slightly.

I narrow my eyes. I can see that Ian is a serious
contender for Star of the Week. Still, Miss Moon
cannot fail to recognize my potential this time.
My natural talent as a pre-teen supermodel is bound
to shine through. Perhaps a talent scout will spot

me and sign me up for London Fashion Week, or put me on the cover of *Vogue* magazine!

Willow said that model scouts are everywhere, just when you least expect it, and you cannot always tell who they might be. It could be anyone. Mrs Mascarpone the school cook, maybe, or Mr Smart the Head, or even Mr Bleecher the caretaker in his spare time. Or maybe not.

Still, I have to stay positive and look on the bright side.

Miss Moon checks her watch. 'Everybody ready?' she asks. 'I am going to collect Class Five.'

Miss Moon ushers us outside the door on the far side of the hall, and we huddle together, waiting.

We hear Class Five file into the hall and take their seats, and then Miss Moon appears in the doorway to tell us it's time. She gives us a big thumbs up and slips inside to introduce the show. Luka's music booms out and Ali's lightshow begins to flash and Ethan is peering into a hand mirror and adding a few last tweaks to his perfectly gelled hair . . . and then, finally, we are on.

It goes like a dream. The crowd gasp as Willow struts along the catwalk in her bubble-wrap ballgown. They watch transfixed as Beth slinks along in her shredded-paper tutu, adding a little pirouette at the end of the catwalk space. By the time Murphy strides out in his newspaper tailcoat the place is

sizzling with excitement, and even Ethan takes things seriously for long enough to get to the end of the catwalk and back without wiggling his bum.

Suddenly, I realize it's me next, with Ian to close.

I step out into the spotlight and try for the catwalk strut, but it is not easy in towering cardboard platforms. I make it to the end of the catwalk and pause for a moment, doing a twirl in case the classroom assistant from Class Five turns out to be a model scout in disguise, and then I am lurching back towards the door, but gracefully of course, because of all the practice I have put in over the last few weeks.

Seriously, I think it may be one of the most exciting moments of my life . . . and as I stagger back out into the corridor I can hear that everyone is cheering. More than cheering . . . they are going crazy!

A slow blush seeps over my cheeks. All the hard work, all the worry and stress and the secret fears that maybe I was destined for a life of wellies and goatherding rather than supermodel stardom . . . all of that is worth it now.

'Hear that?' Murphy grins. 'I think they liked it! Well done, Daizy! And trust Ian to steal the show!'

I blink.

Ian? I peer through the classroom door and see Ian Knox marching back along the catwalk, his recycled-cycle costume flashing and whirring as he goes. Class Five are on their feet, whistling, yelling, and Ian is taking a bow, holding his bicycle-wheel hat steady with one hand.

Ian . . . Ian stole the show.

Not me.

13

There is only one place you can run to if you want to be alone at school in the middle of lesson time, and that is the girls' loos. I clomp along the corridor, wiping the tears away with the back of my hand.

I push the door open and stumble inside, and there to my surprise I find Beth, sitting on the floor beside the waste-paper bin in her shredded-paper tutu, blowing her nose into a handful of scratchy white loo roll.

'What are you doing?'

'Um . . . just checking this stuff out,' she says, holding up the loo roll, looking shifty. 'In case I ever need to make a party dress from it. Or a tutu. Or something. Obviously. What are you doing here?

You should be enjoying your moment of glory, Daizy!'

'Huh,' I mutter. 'Nobody even noticed I'd gone. Ian got all the attention with his flashing lights and bicycle wheels, and Murphy is the hero, really, because he helped so many people with their designs. What did I do? Nothing. I don't think modelling is going to be my Star Quality, Beth. I was rubbish.'

'I bet you weren't,' she says kindly. 'Don't give up the dream, Daizy. I expect it was just the shoes.'

I sit down on the floor beside her.

'Maybe,' I sigh. 'Beth . . . do you think I will ever get a Star of the Week award? Will I ever find my Star Quality?'

'Of course you will,' she says firmly. 'You are one of the most amazing people I know, Daizy Star! Promise me you won't go off to live on the Isle of Muck?'

I bite my lip. That's one thing I can't promise, even though I really, really want to.

'Do you think they have model scouts up there?' I ask.

'Probably,' Beth says. 'Almost definitely.'

And then a big tear rolls down Beth's cheek and plops on to the shredded paper of her skirt.

'Hey, hey!' I protest. 'Don't cry, Beth! We can still be friends, no matter what . . . even if I am living hundreds of miles away on a windswept island. Nothing will change!'

'Everything will change,' Beth snuffles. 'It always does, no matter what people say. Everything's rubbish just now!'

Beth dissolves into floods of tears, hiding her face in her hands.

I blink, horrified.

'Don't cry, Beth!' I whisper. 'Your dress will go all soggy!'

I don't think she cares, though, so I put my arm round her and hold her tight and she cries until there are no more tears left.

'What's wrong?' I ask.

'Everything,' Beth snuffles. 'Just . . . everything!'

Well, I know that feeling, obviously. Everything goes wrong in my life all the time. I just lurch from one disaster to the next, pretty much – it's kind of exhausting.

My friends, though, are always there for me. Beth, Willow and Murphy always listen, always understand, always know what to say and do. And now Beth needs my help. Why didn't I get her to talk to me properly before? I noticed something was wrong – I just didn't notice enough. I have been too wrapped up in my own worries to think about much else.

'Tell me,' I say.

So she does. It turns out that her grandma is ill with one of those old-people illnesses where you keep on forgetting things, like the date and the year and where you live, and even your own name.

'She has been getting worse and worse for ages now,' Beth explains. 'Grandad can't look after her any more, because she kept doing dangerous things like wandering off to the allotment in her nightie

101

and setting fire to the kitchen.'

'Oh, Beth!' I say. 'She was such a cool gran too. Remember when she used to help us make sponge cake, with loads of pink colouring because it was our favourite colour? And let us use that squelchy icing stuff to spell out our names on top.'

'Now she doesn't remember my name at all,' Beth sighs. 'Dad says she needs proper care, and Mum says there was no other option, and Grandad says he will never, ever forgive himself.'

'For what?' I ask.

'For moving her into an old people's home,' Beth says in a small voice. 'The Twilight Years Rest Home.'

'No way!' I gasp. 'I've heard of that place. Where is it?'

'Just along the road from here,' Beth says. 'We walk past it every day on the way to school. It's that big Victorian house with all the ivy and the big wrought-iron gates.'

Beth is right – I must have seen the Twilight Years Rest Home about a million times. It looks kind of dark and forbidding, like something from a horror movie.

I bite my lip.

'It's not fair, Daizy!' Beth goes on. 'We went to see her and she looked all lost and lonely, slumped in a chair half asleep; it was horrible! I mean, they are looking after her OK, but . . . everyone in there seems so sad, so miserable. Like they could die of boredom at any minute.'

I blink. I am not sure if people can actually die of boredom; if they could, I would never have made it through so many numeracy lessons, surely? Still, it might be different when you are old.

'My grandad is really missing her – he's gone all quiet and sad. And Mum and Dad are worried, I know they are. It's just not right, Daizy!'

Beth blows her nose.

'I'm glad you told me,' I say. 'You have to tell your friends when something is wrong, Beth – that's what friends are for! Besides, you, Willow and Murphy have always been there for me, haven't you?'

'I suppose . . .'

'We will think of something,' I tell her. 'Something to liven up the old people's home and make sure your gran and grandad are OK.

103

That's a promise!'

I may have been a hopeless friend lately, but if I have to leave my best mates to be a goatherd on the Isle of Muck, the least I can do is help Beth before I go.

'You're the best, Daizy Star,' she says, hugging me.

I bite my lip. I've just promised Beth to help her gran – but how on earth am I going to do that?

14

I an Knox gets a Star of
the Week award for
having the best costume
in the fashion show, but
I don't even mind any more.
After all, a shy boy who is
brave enough to wear a hat
made from a warped bicycle wheel wired up
with flashing lights . . . well, he probably deserves it.

Besides, I have moved on. My new mission is to
liven up the old people of the Twilight Years Rest
Home so they don't die of boredom, because if
they are happy, Beth will be happy too. I hope.

I start planning right away, because really, there
is no time to spare. Dad has booked a viewing for

the cottage on Muck for next weekend. It turns out that it is not so much a viewing as an actual interview – the island is so small that anyone who wants to live there has to be checked and vetted to make sure they will fit in.

We will catch the afternoon ferry over, view the cottage and then meet the Island Committee in the community hall so they can talk to us all. We will stay overnight and explore a little more the next morning before heading back to the mainland for the long drive home.

Yikes. This is really happening.

I want to say something, argue, explain that my life will be over if we go to live on a windswept rock in the middle of the ocean, but I can't find the words. How can I explain to Mum and Dad that their dream is my nightmare?

As for my sisters and our pact to stick together, it's just not happening. Becca is so sad about Spike she doesn't care any more, and Pixie is actually getting quite excited about the possibility of mermaid sightings.

Typical.

'What kind of an interview is it, exactly?' I ask.

'They want to see what we can bring to the island,' Dad explains. 'There's your mum's nursing skills, my teaching, you three girls with your own unique talents . . . and I've been working on a business plan too – something that will bring in an income. I thought we could focus on one particular thing we do really, really well . . .'

'Such as?' I ask.

I hope it will not be free-range eggs, because I am pretty sure there won't be a Tesco on the Isle of Muck – and how else can I keep Attila, Esmerelda and Cleopatra in business? But no, Dad has other ideas.

'Nettles,' he announces, grinning.

'Nettles?' I echo.

Dad shrugs. 'They are our best crop – a very underrated vegetable, full of iron and vitamins. In time, we can develop our own range of nettle-based ready meals. It's a whole new market, unexplored!'

'There might be a reason for that,' I say.

'Dad,' Pixie chips in politely. 'Everybody hates nettles. They are vile.'

Dad laughs. 'You don't mean that, Pixie,' he says. 'Nettles are the future! Clean, green, super-healthy.'

We are going to be nettle farmers on the Isle of Muck. Seriously. Just when I think it can't get any worse . . .

I decide to focus on something I might actually be able to do something about – helping the residents of the Twilight Years Rest Home.

I talk to Willow and Murphy first, explaining about Beth's gran.

'The oldies at the Twilight Years Rest Home are just along the road from us in Stella Street,' I say. 'Yet we never see them. We never even think about them. But every person in there is probably someone's gran or grandad, right? Maybe their grandchildren live miles and miles away, or maybe they don't have any at all . . . they must be so lonely!'

'So, what can we do about it?' Willow asks.

'We can liven things up,' I say brightly. 'Put on our fashion show! They'll love it!'

'You think?' Murphy asks doubtfully.

'Definitely!' I say. 'The fashion show was cool, everyone said so. Besides, we have the clothes now and we know what to do. It would be easy!'

'Maybe,' Willow shrugs. 'But . . . well, bubble-wrap ballgowns and sweet-wrapper jeans may not be their kind of thing. Wouldn't we be better thinking about what elderly people might actually like?'

I frown. Willow and Murphy could be right, but I cannot let go of the idea. I have another reason I think we should put on the fashion show again, but it's a selfish one – it will mean I get another shot at fame. And that might just save me from life on an offshore island with only a goat for a friend.

'I think they'd like the fashion show,' I say. 'But, I suppose we could think of other things too, things that are more their style.'

'Good plan, Daizy,' Murphy says.

'But . . . what *do* old people like?' I puzzle.

Willow raises an eyebrow. 'I guess you'd better find out.'

I do some research. I start out by asking Beth

what her gran used to like, and
the answer is tea, baking and
pottering around the garden.
Margie Brown next door says she
likes bingo, old-time dancing and

making jam tarts, and Bert Brown,
of course, says
gardening. I
ask everyone
at school to find

out what the oldies they know like
too, and gradually I draw up a list:

bingo
dancing
baking cakes
drinking tea
gardening
chatting
knitting

I come up with a plan, and I think it is a foolproof one. As well as the fashion show, we will have a bingo game, an old-fashioned dance and lots of tea served with homemade cupcakes.

All I have to do now is make sure Year Six – and Miss Moon – agree to help. It takes a while to find the courage, but eventually I manage to put my hand up in the middle of the Numeracy Hour.

'Miss?' I say. 'I have an idea, and I need your help!'

'Oh? What is it, Daizy?'

'I have been thinking,' I say. 'About the Twilight Years Rest Home, just along from the school. I have been worrying about the residents. They are old, and I think they might be very bored and lonely. I think we should try to make friends with them.'

'The Twilight Years Rest Home?' Ethan Miller smirks. 'Don't tell me. It's a home for retired vampires.'

'It is not!' Beth blazes. 'My gran lives there, and she is not a vampire!'

'Sorr-ee,' Ethan says. 'It was a joke! Twilight! Geddit?'

'Quiet, Ethan,' Miss Moon cuts in. 'It's a great idea, Daizy. It would be wonderful to make some links between Stella Street Primary and the Twilight Years Rest Home. I will see what Mr Smart says, and if he is happy I can make a few phone calls, see if we can set something up.'

'Oh!' I blink. 'That would be brilliant, Miss Moon!'

'We should all respect our elders,' she tells the class. 'Senior citizens have lived long lives, worked hard, raised families. They have been through good times and bad. They might be battling with illness, perhaps without friends or family nearby.'

'I've never thought about it like that,' Ethan says.

'Well,' Miss Moon says kindly. 'Not many of us do. But we can think about it now, can't we? Well done, Daizy, for suggesting this!'

'I thought we could put on a show, try to cheer them up.'

Beth is smiling, really smiling, for the first time in weeks. I am pretty sure I can put a smile on the faces of the old folks at the Twilight Years Rest Home too . . . and that would make Beth really happy, I know it would.

It might even put me in the running for a Star of the Week award . . . and more importantly, putting on the fashion show means I have another shot at fame. This time, I will make sure that I am centre stage. All I have to do is invite the press along to our Twilight Years event – and get my photo taken.

Even if there are no actual model scouts hidden away among the nurses and carers of the Twilight Years Rest Home, there might be a few scanning the newspapers for new talent. And my picture will jump out at them, and my woven net-and-brown-paper dress will stun everyone with its beauty and originality.

People will be amazed. 'Who is that girl?' they will ask.

'So fresh-faced, so unusual, so different,' they will say.

'So thoughtful, so kind, so caring,' they will add.

And by the end of the following week, I will be signed up to one of the top modelling agencies and far too busy shooting cover sessions for *Vogue*

magazine to go and live on an island in the middle
of nowhere with no friends, no school and no
custard doughnuts.

It could happen, couldn't it?

# 15

The next day, Miss Moon calls the matron at the Twilight Years Rest Home, who is delighted at the offer of some free entertainment. A date is set for next Monday afternoon – just after our return from the Isle of Muck. We will put on a mini version of the fashion show, along with tea and music, and Bert and Margie from next door will do a bit of a foxtrot. Everyone wants to help, even Ethan, who offers to set up a five-a-side football match for the oldies.

I glare at him. 'Some of them are in their nineties,' I snap. 'Some are in wheelchairs or on Zimmer frames. I want to cheer them up, not finish them off!'

Ethan pulls a face. 'I'll think of something,' he says.

As far as I know, Ethan never thinks of anything but football, mirrors and hair gel, but I suppose there could always be a first time.

A reporter from the local paper has promised to come along, and Miss Moon has asked me to do a short speech to explain about the green fashion show and how everyone at Stella Street Primary would like to help make the Twilight Years Rest Home a happier place.

I promise to come up with something impressive. I don't think that speech-making is actually one of my skills, but I am bound to be able to jot down a few ideas this weekend. After all, it's not as if trudging around the Isle of Muck is going to be ultra-exciting, is it?

'Leave it to me, Miss Moon,' I say.

Then it will be tea and homemade cakes and biscuits, although I think I may actually cheat and buy some custard doughnuts from the bakery. I don't want to take any risks with one of Dad's creations. What if one of the oldies ends up choking to death on a lentil brownie?

Luka has put together a new 1950s/60s soundtrack for the fashion show, using CDs his own grandparents have, but admits he doesn't have a clue what kind of music people would waltz and foxtrot to. I think hard. My sister Becca plays the violin, and she is in the school orchestra. She probably has a couple of classical waltz CDs I can borrow.

Better still, how about a live performance? A plan begins to form in my head.

Becca is still in mourning. Even though Spike keeps phoning the house and asking to speak to her, she won't come to the phone.

'If I could just see her, Daizy,' he hints, whenever I happen to answer. 'Talk to her properly. I'm sure I could make her understand. Do you think you could get her to meet me?'

There is about as much chance of that as of getting Dad to give up on his dreams of nettle farming on the Isle of Muck, but I cannot bring myself to tell Spike that. It is all very stressful.

Playing for the oldies might just cheer Becca up and take her mind off Spike.

'Becca?' I ask her after school. 'Will you come and play the violin at the Twilight Years Rest Home on Monday afternoon? And ask a couple of friends from the orchestra? It's for a really, really good cause!'

Becca sighs dramatically. She has been doing a lot of that lately. I bet she misses Spike as much as he misses her, but I know my sister – she will never admit she was wrong.

'Maybe,' she says, in a tiny, tragic voice.

'Please?' I beg. 'It would mean so much to me. If we really do move to the Isle of Muck, this could be my last ever chance to win a Star of the Week award.'

She rolls her eyes.

'Go on then,' she sighs. 'I expect the teachers would let me, if I explain. They are always saying we need more practice playing to a live audience. I could ask Sophie and Rachel too.'

'You could always ask Spike,' I venture.

'I will never ask him anything again,' Becca

growls. 'He is nothing to me now.' And she bursts into tears.

'Becca,' I say bravely. 'Do you think . . . with Spike . . . well, do you think you could have been just a teeny bit . . . well . . . hasty?'

'If he loved me he would run away to Paris with me,' Becca snuffles.

'I think he does love you,' I tell her. 'He just doesn't want you to live in a cardboard box. He wants you to be safe and happy and not live under a bridge or in a doorway. Becca . . . admit it. It wasn't a very good idea, was it? Do you think you might have been . . . well . . . *wrong*?'

'No way,' Becca sniffs. 'You'll understand when you are older, Daisy.'

I am not sure about that. I don't think I will understand Becca, not even if I live to be 103.

I've been trying to pretend our trip to Muck isn't really happening, but finally the fateful day dawns. Actually, it doesn't. We set off for Scotland at four on Saturday morning, which is practically the middle of the night. Becca, Pixie and I sleep for the first few hours, snuggled in soft blankets in the back of the car, and when we wake up it's eight o'clock and raining hard, and we are at a service station near Stoke-on-Trent.

We eat cereal and drink hot chocolate, and suddenly, it is an hour later and Dad says we have to get a move on because there is only one ferry going to the Isle of Muck today, and missing it is not an option. That's when things start to get stressy, because we hit a traffic jam around Blackburn that brings the whole motorway to a halt.

'Come on!' Dad mutters. 'We have a ferry to catch!' But the rain keeps lashing down and the traffic crawls at a snail's pace.

'I don't want to live in a place where it rains

120

all the time,' I say.

'How do you know it rains all the time?' Pixie asks reasonably. 'We're not even in Scotland yet!'

'I might come off the motorway and take a side road,' Dad says anxiously. 'We have to make it in time for that ferry.'

So we come off the motorway, take a wrong turning and get lost in a place called Oswaldtwistle. In the end we have to go right back on to the motorway again, and  nobody even dares to speak to Dad after that. We are hours behind schedule and unless the car suddenly sprouts wings we are not going to make it to Mallaig by half past two.

'They'll be expecting us on Muck,' Dad worries. 'They're meeting us off the ferry! There are six other families interested in this cottage, you know. If we can't even get ourselves to the island on time, the islanders might decide we are not the right people for their community.'

'If they think that, they are not very understanding,' Mum remarks. 'We can't control the weather or the traffic on the M6, can we?'

We drive on in silence, not even stopping for lunch, and even though we are in Scotland now it is very hard to get excited. Especially when you never wanted to go in the first place.

I have a feeling of impending doom.

We arrive in Mallaig just in time to see the ferry vanish into the cold, misty horizon.

16

'Now what?' Mum sighs as we sit in the car, looking out to sea.

'I will text Hamish,' Dad says decisively. 'He will know what to do.'

So Dad texts his contact on the Isle of Muck, and a text comes back telling us to drive down to the next village and look for a small red fishing boat called *Lady Muck*, which may be able to give us a lift over.

'Hamish will get a message to the fishermen, so they will be expecting us,' Dad says, driving on. 'See how everyone pulls together? This is the place for us, I can feel it in my bones!'

When we reach the village, we see a damp, stony beach stretched beside an iron-grey sea and a red fishing boat moored against the seawall. Dad runs

over to it, waving. He talks for a few minutes to a man in a yellow waterproof hat and then hurries back to us through the driving rain.

'They're ready to leave,' he tells us. 'We can just park the car down on the beach, out of the way.'

'On the beach?' Mum echoes, frowning.

'I think that's what he said,' Dad shrugs, veering off the road and driving down across the dunes. 'He's got quite a strong accent, but I'm getting to grips with it already.'

He parks neatly on the wet shingle and we pile out of the car and trudge back towards the fishing boat. We are bundled aboard and into the tiny cabin as the engines fire and roar and the boat moves slowly out from the quayside. We huddle together in a tiny space that stinks of fish. Rain lashes the cabin windows as the boat lurches through the waves.

Two red-faced fishermen ask Dad why he wants to move to an island.

'The fresh air!' he tells them. 'The wide-open spaces! The freedom!'

'It's no' an easy life, ken?' one of the men says gruffly, and Dad says that actually, his name isn't Ken but Mike, which makes the fishermen laugh and roll their eyes. We clamber ashore two hours later, just as the light is fading. Hamish is waiting for us with a big umbrella that threatens to blow inside out at any minute.

'Welcome to Muck!' he declares. 'It's a shame you can't see it in the daylight, but I know you're going to fall in love with it!'

I know I am not.

Hamish loads us into the back of a jeep, drops our bags off at a cute little guest house and drives a short way along a single-track road. When we get out again, it is pitch-black and we are standing in a

125

muddy field as Hamish squelches forward, leading us by torchlight towards a tiny hut.

It looks very different from the picture of the whitewashed cottage with roses round the door that Mum and Dad fell in love with. It seems smaller, and older, with peeling paint and no sign of roses anywhere.

'Is this it?' Mum asks.

'The picture you saw was taken in the summer,' Hamish admits. 'The cottage has been empty a while. It just needs a little love and attention to be a happy family home again.'

The lights flicker on and we can see that

somebody has placed a vase of wintry branches hung with berries and catkins on the window sill to make it seem more welcoming. 'What happened to the last people?' Mum asks.

Hamish looks shifty. 'They weren't right for Muck,' he says, with a shrug. 'City types, you see. Not everyone is cut out for island living.'

'We are,' Dad says, trying to be chirpy. 'We're going to love it here!'

But the cottage is cold and slightly musty with spiderwebs hiding behind the doorways. We troop upstairs. The floorboards creak beneath our feet and we have to duck to avoid hitting our heads on the sloping attic roof. We peer politely into one, two, three bedrooms.

'Dad?' I ask, alarmed. 'We need four bedrooms, don't we?'

'Yes, we do,' Dad agrees. 'We've talked about this, though – we'd have to look into building an extension.'

'The property is rented,' Hamish points out. 'Any alterations would have to be approved by the Island Committee.'

'How about bunk beds, girls?' Dad grins. 'You and Pixie would like that!'

'Share a room?' I frown.

'With Daizy?' Pixie echoes, faintly horrified.

'We'll talk about it later,' Mum promises, but my heart sinks and I am suddenly homesick for the little bedroom where I have shared so many sleepovers and heart-to-hearts. There would be no sleepovers here, that's for sure. How could my friends even come to visit when the island is so far away? It took us a whole day to get here.

A good clean and a coat of paint would make everything look brighter, but nothing can change the fact that the rooms are tiny and the windows small. So much for more space and freedom – we have more space at home.

'Of course, we would be spending more time outdoors here,' Dad says, reading my mind. 'We'd be on the beach, in the fields, tending the animals, out in the fresh air and sunshine.'

We all turn to look at the window, where rain is hammering against the glass. Fresh air and sunshine seem as unlikely right now as unicorns in the garden.

'Let's head over to the community hall,' Hamish says. 'The committee cannot wait to meet you. There'll be a buffet supper to welcome you – all very informal.'

It doesn't feel very informal, though, when we are sitting in a row on hard wooden chairs, facing the committee. Dad explains all about his plan to make nettles into the next great British supercrop. 'Think of it!' he beams. 'Field after field of rich, green nettles, as far as the eye can see.'

'Hmmm,' Hamish says, looking a little anxious. 'It's certainly an unusual idea.'

Dad passes round samples of nettle super-smoothie and nettle flapjack. The committee nibble and sip politely, exchanging worried glances.

'Let's leave the nettles aside for now,' a bearded man says. 'Do you think you and your family have the qualities needed to survive a long, hard island winter, Mr Star? It's not always an easy life for ex-townies.'

'We want to be islanders,' Dad says. 'We want the space to keep our livestock. We want to follow our dream. We are nettle farmers! We are country people trapped in the town – we can't wait for the long, hard winters! We don't care about things like TV shows and oven chips. We prefer nettle stew!'

I glare at Dad. He is the only person I know who can even swallow nettle stew, let alone prefer it to oven chips.

'What about you, Mrs Star?' an elderly lady dressed in tweed enquires. 'Is this what you want too?'

'It could be,' Mum replies carefully. 'We are looking for a challenge. Something new. To be a part of a real community – find a slower pace of life.'

'You think life is easy here?' the elderly lady frowns.

'No!' Mum says quickly. 'That's not what I meant.

130

We just want to step out of the rat race and find a place we can belong.'

The committee members nod and smile and shuffle their papers.

'How about you youngsters?' Hamish asks. 'What are you looking for from life on Muck?'

'I'm looking for mermaids,' Pixie says firmly. 'I wouldn't mind a dolphin or two, but it's mermaids, mainly.'

'Er . . . of course,' Hamish nods. He looks at Becca.

'I'm looking for rain,' my big sister says. 'And solitude. And time to heal my broken heart.'

Hamish looks nervous. 'Lovely,' he says, then fixes his gaze on me. 'What about you, dear? What are you hoping to get from life on Muck?'

For a moment, I panic. There is nothing I want from this place, except perhaps a return trip to the mainland, but I don't want to be rude. Even tonight, in the dark, in the middle of a downpour, sitting in a draughty hall, I can see that the Isle of Muck is probably OK, in a rugged, outdoorsy kind of way. If I was the kind of girl who wanted to go sailing or fishing or pony riding, I might even like it. If I could picture a future of nettle-picking and chicken-feeding and goat-grooming, then maybe this would be the perfect place to do it. But I can't.

I am never going to be the kind of girl who is happy in wellies and raincoat, collecting seaweed from the beach for Dad's latest revolting soup.

'Actually, I am planning to be the first pre-teen supermodel,' I say with confidence. 'I will travel the world and be on the cover of all the coolest magazines. I expect I will be spotted by a model scout any day now, so don't worry, I won't actually be here much. I might come back to visit occasionally, when I am not in London or Paris or New York. For birthdays and Christmas, perhaps.'

The islanders are staring at me open-mouthed, as if they have never seen a pre-teen supermodel before. Well, they probably haven't. Hamish snorts with laughter, but I don't care – what would he know about fashion, anyway?

Mum, Dad, Becca and Pixie are gawping a little too, but it is best that they know the truth about my plans for the future. They may need some time to adjust, but they'll be glad in the end when I am rich and famous and able to buy them a big mansion with its very own nettle farm attached.

'Daizy has a very vivid imagination,' Dad says smoothly. 'She will be an asset to the island, I promise you. Do tell me about the schools; the girls are so looking forward to meeting their new classmates!'

I glare at Dad. I already have the best classmates ever, and the most amazing teacher. I do not care a bit about the schools on Muck.

'We have a thriving primary school,' Hamish says proudly. 'There are eight pupils at the moment. Pixie and Daizy would bring the numbers up to ten!'

'Ten in the whole *school*?' I gasp.

'Older children, like Becca here, go to school on the mainland.'

'The mainland?' Mum echoes. 'You mean she'd have to catch a ferry over every morning and one

133

back at night? It's a two-hour journey!'

'Indeed,' Hamish says. 'That would never work. No, high-school students board on the mainland during term time. Much more sensible.'

'Board?' Becca says slowly. 'As in . . . boarding school?'

'Exactly!'

'Great,' Becca says flatly.

The committee look pleased – I don't think they have come across my big sister's sarcasm before.

'So,' Hamish says. 'I think that's all we need for now. Time for a bowl of warm soup, a wee cup of tea and some homemade shortbread. Listen to Angus on the bagpipes, perhaps!'

'Thank you, all of you,' Dad grins, shaking hands with Hamish and the other islanders. 'You've made us feel very welcome!'

I sigh. They have made us feel welcome, I suppose. Maybe I need to give this whole island thing a chance, if only for the sake of Buttercup, Attila the Hen, Esmerelda and Cleopatra. At least I know they'd have a better life here.

Hamish hands me a bowl of grey, steaming soup.

'Um . . . what kind of soup is it?' I ask politely.

'Chicken,' he tells me. 'One of my own hens, fresh in the pot today!'

I drop my bowl on to the cold stone floor, and it shatters into about a million little pieces, spattering soup everywhere.

## 17

I lie awake all night in the guest room I am sharing with my sisters, picturing my life as a nettle-farmer's daughter.

When I finally do get to sleep, I have nightmares of my supermodel debut, prancing along a catwalk that soars like a cliff above a treacherous sea, wearing a dress made of nettles and towering shoes made of fishbones. I wake up in a twist of duvet, breathless, heart pounding.

It is late morning and pale golden sunshine floods in through the curtains. We get dressed, eat a big family breakfast of porridge and cream and scrambled egg, and wrap up warm to walk

over to look at the cottage again.

In the daylight, it seems brighter, prettier, more like the picture Mum and Dad fell in love with.

'It's perfect,' Dad sighs. 'I know we can be happy here!'

'Perhaps,' Mum says. 'Are you sure this is what you want, Mike?'

'I'm sure,' Dad says, and my heart sinks as I watch my own hopes and dreams crumble away.

'Shouldn't we be starting for the mainland, Dad?' I plead, trying to drag them back to reality. 'We have such a long drive home. Don't forget that the fashion show at the Twilight Years Rest Home is tomorrow afternoon. I will need my beauty sleep if I am going to be spotted as the first pre-teen supermodel.'

'Ha, ha, Daizy,' Dad says. 'You have a great sense of humour!'

'I am deadly serious,' I say coldly.

'You are?' he gulps. 'Er . . . of course you are. Look, Hamish will take us back to the mainland as soon as we are ready. Just be patient a bit longer, while we look around in the daylight.'

'It's our future,' Mum says, and I bite my tongue

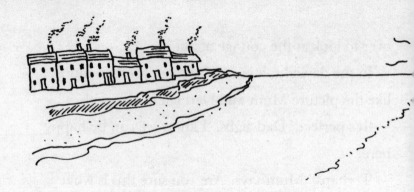

because it is not the future I had in mind, not at all.

I look out across the beach at the silver-blue ocean that stretches on forever, and I think of Beth and Willow and Murphy Malone, and Miss Moon, and even stupid Ethan Miller. My eyes blur with tears.

When we finally do leave, it takes hours for Hamish to run us back to the mainland in his motor boat, and there is lots of chat about solar panels and windmills and ferries and which kids go to high school on the mainland. Through it all, Becca stares out to sea, her eyes wide and tragic, while Pixie scans the surf for signs of mermaids.

'Look at that amazing sunset, kids!' Dad sighs, but all I can think of is the long drive home and how wrecked I will be feeling for the fashion show tomorrow. I will try to remember to put a couple

of cucumber slices over my eyes when I finally do crawl into bed, to make sure I wake up feeling bright-eyed and sparkly.

Hamish delivers us safely to the quayside and shakes everybody's hand. He says it was a pleasure to have us on Muck and that the Island Committee will be in touch in a few days to tell us whether we will be chosen to join the community. 'We still have one more family left to interview, but we should have a decision soon. I'm hoping it will be good news for you.'

'Thanks, Hamish,' Dad grins.

Hamish waves and motors back out into the velvet darkness, and we walk along towards the shingle beach where we parked the car.

'Isn't the sea a bit higher than yesterday?' Mum

asks. 'I can't quite see the car . . .'

Dad frowns. 'It just looks a little different in the dark. Don't worry, I know exactly where we are. See this big rock? We are parked just down from it.'

Dad points into the darkness.

'I still can't see it,' Mum says, a note of anxiety creeping into her voice. 'Pixie, where's that torch?'

Pixie shines her torch out over the dunes. The beach and the shingle have vanished . . . there is nothing to be seen but a shimmering expanse of ink-black sea.

And then we spot the little red saloon car sticking up out of the water, the surf lapping at the windows.

'Oh dear,' Becca says, smirking.

It is the first time I've seen her smile in weeks.

18

It is not easy to explain to the local policeman that our car is underwater, but Dad manages it somehow.

'Och, that old abandoned car?' he says. 'It was reported this morning. Old Tam is bringing his tractor up to tow it away.'

'It's not abandoned,' Dad argues. 'I just parked it on the beach!'

'Whatever for?' the policeman sighs. 'We have a car park!'

'The fishermen told me to,' Dad mutters. 'At least, I thought they did. It's a very strong accent.'

The policeman shakes his head.

By the time Old Tam appears with his tractor, the high tide has receded and the car sits dripping on the shingle, a few lengths of seaweed dangling from the wipers. Old Tam tows it up on to the road, but things are looking bad. I fight back the tears. My chances of getting back to Brightford in time for the fashion show are somewhere around zero . . . or possibly less.

'What are we going to do?' I whisper.

'We're in the AA,' Dad says, still hopeful. 'Let's give them a call. We might still make it back in time.'

But not even the AA man can rescue our car, although he does poke about under the bonnet with his flashlight and rescue a large brown crab, still wriggling. He shakes his head despairingly, and announces that the car is well and truly dead. I start to panic about the fashion show, but luckily the AA man arranges a replacement car for Dad to drive us home. After yet more waiting, we finally start the

long drive home at two o'clock in the morning. Could this trip have been more of a disaster?

It's eleven the next morning by the time we finally get back home. I feel terrible – I've hardly slept and I keep thinking about the awful life that looms ahead of me on Muck . . . but I have to make the fashion show. I have just over an hour to get ready and get to school before the class are due to leave to set things up at the Twilight Years Rest Home.

'I feel like death,' Becca says. 'I could sleep for a week.'

'You can't! You are supposed to be playing the violin this afternoon for the oldies at the Twilight Years Rest Home!'

'Daizy, you can't seriously expect –'

'I do seriously expect,' I snap. 'You have to be there, Becca. The oldies need you. I need you! You promised!'

'But –'

'But nothing!' I say. 'A promise is a promise. The show must go on!'

'Daizy,' Becca says, her voice concerned. 'You're

143

not still hoping to be spotted by a model scout, are you? Because I don't want to spoil your dreams, and you know I think you are the coolest, cutest little sister in the world, apart from Pixie here, who is just as gorgeous, but I really don't think you should get your hopes up. Modelling is a tough career to break into . . .'

I slam my hands over my ears.

Lots of top models probably have this trouble – people doubting their Star Quality. Becca doesn't mean any harm – she is tired and fed up and sad about Spike, and she is only worrying in the first place because she cares about me. I refuse to be discouraged.

Then I look in
the living-room
mirror. My hair
is sticking up
in three or
four different
directions and
there are dark
smudges under my

eyes. This is not good.

'It's not about me,' I tell Becca, and this is news even to me. 'I don't care about the modelling thing, not really. I just can't let Beth down!'

Becca raises an eyebrow.

'OK, OK,' she groans. 'I understand. It's a friendship thing, right? Well . . . fine. Let's do this. Go and shower, Daizy Star!'

I leg it up the stairs, jump in the shower and let the warm water wash all traces of Muck away, then I pull on clean clothes, drag a comb through my hair. There is no time to spare. I need to get to school now.

When I gallop down the stairs again, Mum and Dad have crashed out on the sofa and Pixie is asleep in an armchair, but Becca is ironing her uniform for the violin recital later on. She may be a gloomy, heart-broken Goth, who hasn't slept for twenty-four hours, but I know I can count on her.

'I wrote you a note,' she whispers. 'So you don't get into trouble with Miss Moon.'

I wonder what Becca actually wrote.

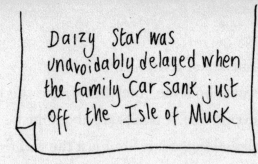

Daizy Star was unavoidably delayed when the family car sank just off the Isle of Muck

'We were meant to bring in cakes for the tea dance,' I whisper back. 'I forgot, but –'

'Sorted,' she says, handing me a foil-wrapped package. 'Dad's nettle flapjacks. They didn't go down too well on Muck – there are quite a lot left.'

'Er . . . thanks, Becca.' I give my big sister a hug.

'Can you feed the animals on your way out?' she asks. 'Bert and Margie were looking after them, but they expected us back last night. I don't think they've been fed today. See you at Twilight Towers, OK?'

I hurry over to the chicken run.

'You needn't look so pleased with yourself,' I say to Attila as I scatter the food. 'There is no Tesco on the Isle of Muck, and I have seen exactly what happens to hens who don't lay eggs . . .'

Attila blinks and ruffles her wings, as if she is the cleverest hen in the universe and not a possible candidate for homemade chicken soup.

The last forty-eight hours have been the worst of my whole, entire life . . . and now I have to go into school and pretend that everything is fine. I want the day to go well for the old people at the Twilight Years Rest Home. I want them to enjoy the fashion show and I want them to enjoy their tea and cakes and get all misty-eyed at the dance display and the live orchestra. I even picture one or two of them getting up to join in, waltzing creakily round the room while dreaming of happy days gone by.

Mostly, though, I want today to be a success for Beth. I want her to stop worrying about her gran, to make her see that the Twilight Years Rest Home can be a lively, happy place.

I would like to be a pre-teen supermodel, sure, and I wouldn't mind a Star of the Week award, but more than any of that, I want to do something good for Beth – perhaps for the very last time.

'Hey,' I tell Buttercup. 'This time next month, you might be my only friend.' The trip to Muck was a bit of a disaster, but Dad was still talking all the way home about island life. And Mum was joining in. The future is not looking good.

147

Buttercup has stopped nuzzling my neck and started trying to get my school bag open. I think she has caught a whiff of the nettle flapjacks, so I give her one of them on the basis that the oldies are probably not going to miss it. I ruffle her ears and pull the chicken-run gate closed behind me.

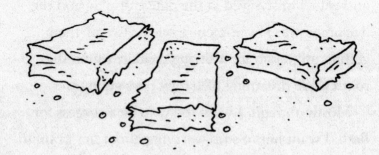

## 19

I head off to school, half running. All the way,
I have an uneasy feeling that I am being
followed, but every time I look back over my
shoulder, there is nobody to be seen. There is one
reason why someone might follow me, of course.
It is unlikely, but Willow did say that model scouts
were everywhere and that often they just spot
people in the street.

It could happen.

Maybe I don't even have to change into my
potato-netting-and-feed-sack party dress to show
my potential. Perhaps my Star Quality just shines
through? I find myself walking extra tall, flicking
my hair and adding the faintest wiggle as I sashay
along the pavement.

I am getting a crick in my neck, but I don't care because I am almost certain now that I am being watched. I look back again, just in time to see something dart out of sight behind a hedge. I fix a dazzling smile on my face and strut towards the school gates.

Maybe – just maybe – someone will call my name and I will be saved from a life of nettle stew and tartan vests on the Isle of Muck. My future will roll out before me like a red carpet, and I will step up to the challenge and stride out in my cardboard wedge heels, or possibly something slightly lower and not made out of string and old boxes.

Just as I get to the school gates, somebody nudges my elbow gently, and my heart thuds. I look round, and the last shreds of dream fall away.

'Meeehhhh . . .'

Buttercup the goat butts her head in under the flap of my school bag and gulps down a couple of nettle flapjacks, still wrapped in silver foil.

'Nooo! Buttercup, what are you doing here?!' I exclaim.

Just then the bell rings out for the end of morning

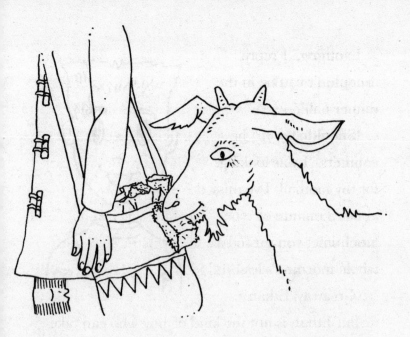

lessons, and in the distance I can see the dinner hall filling up with noisy, hungry pupils. There is no time now to take Buttercup home again – we are supposed to be setting off for the Twilight Years Rest Home as soon as everyone finishes eating.

'Bad girl,' I tell her. 'You could get me into all kinds of trouble!'

I blink. It is clearly a day for trouble, because Ethan Miller is sauntering across the empty playground, a football under his arm. I drag Buttercup out of sight behind the school bins.

'Hey!' he yells. 'What are you doing, Daizy Star?'

'Nothing,' I reply. 'Shouldn't you be in the dinner hall?'

'Shouldn't you?' he counters. 'I was looking for my football. I've missed about a minute of lunchtime; you missed a whole morning's lessons.'

'Go away, Ethan!'

But Ethan is not the kind of boy who can take a hint. He walks over, grinning broadly. 'It's your big day today, right?' he says. 'Your special show for the vampire OAPs.'

'Don't call them that!' I huff.

'I know, I know,' Ethan says. 'It's a joke, Daizy. You are doing a really good thing for the oldies – you've really made me think.'

'I have?'

'Definitely,' he says. 'All those poor old guys who can't kick a ball around any more. Tragic.'

'You have a one-track mind, Ethan Miller,' I snap. 'Football, football, football.'

'What else is there?' he laughs. 'So, Daizy . . . why are you hiding behind the bins?'

'I am not hiding!' I bluff, nudging Buttercup out of sight. 'I am just . . . looking for something.'

Ethan tilts his head to one side. 'Is it . . . a goat?' he asks brightly. 'Because you may not have noticed, but there is actually one just behind you, with its nose in your school bag.'

'Buttercup!' I hiss. 'Stop it! Those flapjacks are for the old folks!'

'Are goats allowed at school?' Ethan wonders.

'No!' I huff. 'And it is your fault, Ethan Miller. You gave me the stupid thing. She is very cute, but very naughty, and she is obsessed with nettle flapjacks. What am I going to do?'

Ethan is a bit of a goat expert, actually. His uncle has a goat farm and that's how come Ethan thought he would give me a goat for Christmas. It was supposed to be part of my fundraising project for Malawi, except that you cannot really parcel up a goat and send it to Africa, can you? Especially a goat like Buttercup, because she would chew through the wrapping paper in ten seconds flat.

So Buttercup stayed with me, and she is probably the reason Dad hatched his crazy plan to be a farmer.

Ethan Miller has ruined my life, and he doesn't even know it.

'I need to take her home, but we're supposed to set off for the rest home right after lunch.'

'Yup,' Ethan says. 'You won't have time. We could just take her with us – it's only a little way along the road, right? We can hide her for now in the caretaker's shed, then I'll double back and fetch her and tie her to a tree in the grounds. Their gardens are a jungle of grass and weeds and stuff. She'll love it, and she'd be doing them a favour!'

'Isn't that kind of risky?'

Ethan squares his shoulders and grins. 'Obviously,' he says. 'But for you, Daisy . . . I'll do it.'

'Er . . . thank you,' I say. 'I think.'

'Daisy!' Miss Moon exclaims. 'You're here! We were so worried you would miss the show, and after all the hard work you've put in!'

She reads the note Becca scribbled for me, but

wisely, does not ask for details. Willow, Beth and Murphy swarm round me, asking about the Isle of Muck. I fix a grin on to my face. 'It was grim, but let's not talk about it right now. C'mon – we have a show to put on!'

We gather up costumes and props and boxes of home-baked scones and prettily iced cupcakes, and set off along Stella Street to the Twilight Years Rest Home. Ethan walks beside Miss Moon, then drops behind, waving and winking at me in a very scary way.

'Ooh!' Willow shrieks. 'Did you see that? Ethan Miller winked at me!'

'It was me he was winking at,' Beth sighs. 'Anyone could see that.'

'I think he had something in his eye,' Murphy says.

'Let's ask him,' Willow insists. 'Oh. Where has he gone? He was here a minute ago!'

But Ethan has vanished, hopefully back to school to rescue Buttercup. He is still missing as the matron from Twilight Years shows us to the big hall where the fashion show will take place, but I'm not sure if anyone has noticed except me. Staging blocks from the school have been delivered to build the catwalk, and tables, chairs and boxes of crockery huddle round the edges waiting to be unpacked and arranged.

'Year Six,' Miss Moon says briskly. 'Let's get to work!'

Soon the hall is all ready and Luka has his soundtrack of 50s and 60s tunes playing. Bert and Margie from next door have arrived, Margie in a startling lime-green sequinned dress.

'I won the Brightford Foxtrot Trophy in this frock in nineteen sixty-two,' she tells us, doing a little twirl. 'I thought it would liven things up!'

Margie tries to whirl me round the floor in a waltz, but I have tied on my cardboard platforms and I can barely stand, let alone dance.

We are putting the final touches to our own costumes when Ethan appears, with twigs in his hair and a big roll of paper under his arm.

'Mission accomplished,' he says.

'What mission?' Miss Moon asks. 'Where have you been, Ethan?'

Ethan grins. 'I forgot something, Miss,' he says. 'Had to go back for it.'

'What did you forget?' Miss Moon frowns.

*Please, please, do not let him tell her it was a runaway goat.*

Ethan grins and takes out the roll of paper from under his arm. 'I made a table football game for all the old blokes who can't get out on to a football pitch any more!'

He unrolls the paper to reveal a huge picture of a football pitch, complete with stands filled with painted supporters in old-fashioned hats and scarves. Ethan unpacks the players, two teams of cardboard cut-out figures dressed in baggy shorts and stripy tops, plus a couple of dice and a tennis ball painted to look like a football.

'Ethan!' Miss Moon breathes. 'This is amazing!

You should have asked before going back to the school to fetch it – you can't just run around the streets on your own – but, well, I can see why you did it. You have put a lot of thought and effort into this. Very well done!'

'It was nothing,' Ethan says modestly. 'I know how I would feel if I was too old and creaky to kick a ball around any more. It was something Daizy said that got me thinking, and I decided to make a game the oldies really could play.'

Just then there's a murmur of chatter and the squeak of wheelchairs and Zimmer frames, and Miss Moon herds us all out of a side door as the old folks come in and take their seats.

'Did you get Buttercup?' I whisper.

'Tied to a tree,' Ethan says, wriggling into his cola-can vest. 'I used a double knot. She's happy. Trust me.'

Hmmm. I am not sure that trusting Ethan Miller could ever be a good plan, but right now I have no choice.

20

Ali dims the lights and Miss Moon ushers us all into a line, ready to step up on to the catwalk. The fashion show – take two – is ready to roll.

'Shouldn't you be out front, Daizy?' Miss Moon whispers. 'You did get your speech ready, didn't you? Explaining about the fashion show?'

My cheeks flush scarlet and I go cold all over. With all the chaos and drama of the weekend, I completely forgot to write a speech. Now, put on the spot, my mind is a blank. My tummy flips over with fear.

'I . . . I forgot,' I whisper, mortified.

Miss Moon sighs. 'Well, never mind. We'll do without. No time to worry about it now – I'm sure it will all be fine.'

She nods to Luka, who launches into his soundtrack, and my classmates step out through the door and on to the catwalk, one by one.

Peering through into the hall, though, I can see that we needed that intro speech. The old folks seem a little confused. They frown at Willow's bubble-wrap ballgown and Beth's shredded-paper tutu, and look slightly shocked at Murphy's sweet-paper jeans and newspaper tailcoat. One old lady jumps back and drops her knitting at the sight of Ian Knox in his flashing bicycle-wheel hat.

I look down at my orange potato-netting top, woven with hay and dandelions and feathers from Attila the Hen. I look at the feed-sack skirt that is really just printed paper pleated into a packing-tape waistband, and the towering shoes made of string and cardboard, and I know that they will hate it. A feeling of dread rises inside me as I listen for my cue.

'Go, Daizy!' Miss Moon says, and I am through the door, tottering up the steps and on to the catwalk, wobbling slightly on my platform shoes.

Beth's gran is sitting right in the middle of the

front row, looking totally confused. One old man
has fallen asleep and is snoring softly, and the care
assistants look slightly bored.

It's all my fault. This fashion show was never
going to appeal to a bunch of oldies, especially when
they haven't got a clue what's going on. If I could
just think of something to say – something to explain
it all, make the oldies smile – I could still save the
day. But I'm too tired from the all-night drive.
My mind is dull, my tongue is tied. I cannot think
of a single thing.

Three figures appear in the open doorway at
the back of the hall – Becca and two of her friends
from orchestra. My big sister grins and gives me a
silent thumbs up, then moves quietly to the side of
the hall.

That's when it all goes wrong. Another familiar face appears in the doorway – a long, sad-eyed face with a beard and horns.

Buttercup trots down the aisle, bleating plaintively and trailing a frayed rope. She leaps up on to the catwalk and skids right to my side, and I have no choice but to grab her rope and step out bravely as though I planned to strut along with a goat at my side the whole time.

I have the attention of the audience now, all right.

I hold my head high, keeping in time to the music, but just as I approach the end of the catwalk I hear a sickening rip. A rush of cool air hits me and a gasp of horror rises from the audience.

Buttercup has torn a huge mouthful out of my pleated feed-sack skirt and is chewing it with enthusiasm. I am sashaying along the catwalk with my knickers on show, and of course, they are the faded pink polka dot frilly ones I have had since I was seven years old.

Panic grips me. I am trapped in the spotlight, unable to move, my mouth frozen into an icy grin.

What would Kate Moss do? I know the answer

to that, of course. She would carry on, smiling and tossing her hair. I take a deep breath and vow to do the same. All I have to do is twirl, turn and totter my way back to the end of the catwalk, but it feels impossible.

I sway on my stupid cardboard platform shoes, stumble and promptly fall over, right in front of Beth's gran. Buttercup takes another big bite out of my skirt, clearly tasting goat feed on the paper sacking.

I look up into the spotlight and tears mist my eyes. I have fallen flat on my face on the catwalk in front of thirty elderly people who can see my knickers and, oh yes, there is a goat eating my dress.

Suddenly, I am aware that three figures are standing behind me in the spotlight: Willow, Beth and Murphy.

'We have brought the earth to her knees!' Murphy declares in a loud, clear voice. 'Our greed is eating her away! We have made the earth cry with our greed and destruction!'

I look at Murphy. I have no idea what he is talking about, but it sounds good. He is making it look as though the whole falling-over thing was meant to happen, as though Buttercup's attack on the feed-sack skirt was planned.

'It is time we looked after the earth,' Murphy goes on. 'Time we stopped wasting her resources. We need to recycle, reuse, rediscover what life is all about.'

Willow and Beth lean down and untie my shoes, helping me to my feet. Murphy takes Buttercup by the collar, and Beth's gran leans up and hands me a crochet shawl to use as a skirt.

'We need to learn to share,' Murphy says.
'We need to treat the earth gently, tread softly,
support each other, join hands and walk together
into the future.'

Beth and Willow lead me away along the
catwalk, hobbling slightly. A few of the old people
in the audience clap uncertainly, but my face burns
with shame. The fashion show is a disaster, and I
am the biggest flop of all.

Right now, life as a hermit on the Isle of Muck
is looking pretty good.

21

I would like to die of shame, but there is no time
to waste on self-pity. I struggle back
into my school uniform and Beth and
Willow drag me into the fray
to help pour tea and serve
cupcakes to the oldies.

'Get over it,' Becca tells me
harshly, tuning up her violin
ready for the dance demonstration.
'Nobody ever died of embarrassment, Daizy. Most
of the old folks are pretty short-sighted – I bet they
didn't see your knickers at all.'

'Oh, we did, dear,' an old lady giggles. 'Pink
with frills and polka dots, weren't they? Wouldn't
mind a pair of those myself!'

I cringe.

'See?' I hiss. 'I will never get over this, Becca. At least nobody turned up from the newspaper. It is a good job we are going to live on an island in the middle of nowhere soon, because I will never be able to show my face around here again.'

'Maybe it is all for the best,' Becca agrees. 'There is nothing here for me now, either. Not since Spike cast me off like a worn-out shoe and left me heartbroken and alone.'

'Men are nothing but trouble,' one of the old ladies nearby chips in. 'You're better off without them, dear.'

'Nonsense,' a man with a white handlebar moustache chimes in. 'Not all men are rotters, you know!'

'Young people today have no sense of romance,' another oldie adds. 'If he really loved you, he would find a way of telling you.'

As if by magic, right at that moment, the doors at the back of the hall swing open and Spike walks in carrying his cello, his long black coat flapping around him. I answered the phone the last time he called and I just happened to mention about the show at the Twilight Years Rest Home, and how Becca would be playing the violin . . .

'Spike!' Becca says, her eyes filling with tears. 'What are you doing here?'

The old ladies nudge each other, scandalized. Spike's green fringe and pierced lip can be a little alarming, until you get used to them.

'That's him!' they whisper. 'The rotter!'

Spike pulls out a huge bunch of velvety-red roses and offers them to Becca.

'I have come to take you away from all this,' he says. 'Run away with me to Paris, or Berlin, or New York, Becca. I am sorry. I was wrong and you were right – we have to be together, even if it means living in a cardboard box under the Eiffel Tower.'

'Ooooh!' the old ladies coo. 'This is better than *Eastenders*!'

'No, no, I'm sorry,' Becca protests. 'I could never have left Mum and Dad and Daizy and Pixie; it was a crazy idea. But when you said that . . . well, I thought you didn't want to be with me any more!'

'Of course I do!' Spike says. 'If you go to live on the Isle of Muck, I will phone you every day and send text messages and emails and I will come up to visit every other weekend, even if it means getting a rowing boat for my birthday. Nothing can keep us apart, Becca!'

'Oh, Spike!' my sister breathes.

'Oh, Becca!'

'Oh, yuck,' I whisper under my breath as they fall into each other's arms and make soppy, sighing, kissy noises. Becca's orchestra friends strike up a slushy tune and the oldies start to clap and cheer, and I realize that this little slice of real-life romance has cheered them up far more than our bungled fashion show.

I guess I will have to accept that I may not be the world's first pre-teen supermodel after all. I am clumsy and accident-prone with a sense of style only my best friends could ever understand. As for being pretty, I think it is safe to say that my only true admirer is Buttercup. Sadly, goats do not buy magazines or clothes, so my modelling future could be bleak. I sigh and pick up a cupcake to console myself.

Ethan sidles up to the cake table and says into my ear, 'Cheer up, Daizy. Buttercup is safe now. I found a new bit of rope and tied her to a tree, and Beth's grandad showed me a special knot so I am pretty sure she won't escape this time.'

'Yeah, right,' I huff. 'I have never been so embarrassed, EVER!'

He laughs. 'Oh, yes, I meant to say . . . cool knickers, Daizy!'

I glare at him, and the smile slides from his face.

'That was my big moment, Ethan,' I snap. 'It

is all ruined now, and all because of you!'

'Me?' Ethan frowns.

'Well, you didn't tie Buttercup up properly before. And you gave her to me in the first place, and that's what got Dad thinking, and now we are going to live on the Isle of Muck to make nettle flapjacks, and I will never see my friends again!'

'Seriously?' Ethan says.

'Seriously.'

'I'll miss you, Daizy,' he says, going a little bit pink.

'Well, I won't miss you!'

I turn my back – I've had enough of Ethan Miller. Luckily, at that moment, Becca and Spike and their friends start playing, and Bert and Margie begin their dance display. It is even better than I imagined, because a couple of the oldies really do join in, and everyone is smiling and sipping tea and swaying in time with the music.

Afterwards, we all get chatting, the oldies and the schoolkids, the teachers and the care assistants, Bert and Margie, Beth's grandad, everyone.

I talk to Beth's gran about making apple pies and

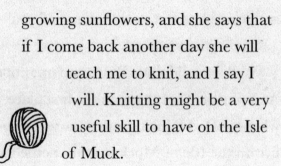

growing sunflowers, and she says that if I come back another day she will teach me to knit, and I say I will. Knitting might be a very useful skill to have on the Isle of Muck.

Even though she doesn't remember who I am, I can see she is happy, and Beth's grandad is happy too. He is telling the Twilight Years matron that he would like to clear the grounds up a bit and make a nice garden round the house for the oldies to enjoy.

'I used to have an allotment,' he explains. 'We worked on it together, Edie and me. I thought, well, what if I do some gardening with Edie right here? And the other residents too? Grow some flowers and vegetables? They might like that!'

'They might!' the matron agrees. 'I haven't been here long, but I can see the grounds have been badly neglected. Any help would be wonderful!'

Over in the corner, Ethan is showing a group of elderly men how to play his table football game, and there are lots of cheers and clinking of teacups whenever a goal is scored. I have to admit that

Ethan's idea seems to be a hit.

By the end of the afternoon, a whole lot of plans have been made. Becca is going to get the orchestra to come in and play now and again, and Bert and Margie have agreed to run dance classes on a Monday afternoon for residents who are mobile enough to take part, and Margie is talking about a weekly bingo evening too.

Miss Moon is going to arrange for a group of children to come in every week to read and chat and talk to the oldies about the past, and there will be occasional classes on knitting, baking and jam making too, with everyone learning from each other.

Nobody asks me to put on another fashion show, but I try not to mind about that. And I try not to mind that very probably I won't be here to help with any of it; I will be miles away, tending my nettles on a windswept rock.

'I can't thank you enough for what you have done today,' the matron says as we are leaving. 'You have done more to liven up the residents in one afternoon than we can do in months. You've been like a breath of fresh air.'

Miss Moon smiles. 'Well, Beth's gran is living here now,' she explains. 'The whole idea came about when Beth's friend Daizy found that out. So, we have Daizy Star to thank for all of this!'

My cheeks burn, but I cannot stop smiling as the matron shakes my hand.

'Thank you, Daizy,' she says. 'You are a very caring, thoughtful girl. You have given us some good ideas too – there will be one or two changes from now on at the Twilight Years Rest Home!'

The whole afternoon has been a big success, even if I did mess up a little. My best friends were there for me when I needed them, which makes me feel very happy inside.

'Beth, Willow,' I say. 'You are the best mates ever, I swear. Murphy Malone, you are the coolest. Your speech saved my bacon back there.'

I won't find friends like them on the Isle of Muck.

22

Mr & Mrs Star
17 Silver Street
Brightford

MUCK

Five days later, a brown envelope with an Isle of Muck postmark comes flopping through the letterbox. Dad shouts for everyone to gather round, and I see his hands are shaking as he holds the envelope.

'Our future lies within,' he says, his eyes shining, and I know that he wants to live on a far-flung island and be an organic nettle farmer very much indeed. 'Wide open spaces, sandy beaches, perfect sunsets . . .'

'Torrential rain,' Becca says. 'Tartan scarves and

bagpipe music. Haggis. Boarding school. No more custard doughnuts.'

I think my big sister has gone off the idea of living on Muck, now she and Spike are back together.

'Open it, Mike,' Mum says. 'Put us out of our misery.'

Dad tears open the envelope and takes out the letter.

' "*Thoroughly enjoyed meeting your delightful family . . .*"' he reads out. ' "*Would be an asset to the island . . .*"'

Then his face falls. ' "*However,*"'  he continues, ' "*we were not convinced that nettle farming is a viable project . . . some concerns that you were a little idealistic about island life . . . sadly, on this occasion, we have decided to offer the smallholding to another family . . .*"'

He blinks. 'I don't believe it! We were meant for that cottage! We were meant for Muck!'

'Seemingly not,' Mum says gently.

176

'I didn't like it, anyway,' Becca shrugs.

'It rained a lot,' Pixie chips in. 'I think that might have put off the mermaids.'

'It's probably freezing in winter,' I say. 'Too cold for nettles.'

Dad just shakes his head.

'Well,' he sighs. 'Looks like we are going to be stuck in the town for a little while yet.'

'Yay!!!' Becca squeals, and Pixie joins in, and Mum sighs and says she is secretly very relieved.

Me, I just hug Dad hard, because I know what it is like to have your hopes and dreams smashed to little pieces. It happens to me all the time.

Slowly, life gets back to normal.

Dad has joined Beth's grandad and Bert from next door in creating a garden from the jungly grounds of the Twilight Years Rest Home. There will be a veggie garden big enough for all of them to take whatever they need, and plenty left over for the Twilight Years kitchens, as well as pretty flower borders where the oldies can sit out and enjoy the sunshine once the weather warms up.

It will be a Community Garden, shared between old and young alike.

Miss Moon has organized squads of pupil volunteers to go in after school and help with the digging, but the real hero has been Buttercup. She has chewed, munched and gnawed her way through a jungle of weeds and brambles, clearing the ground better than any strimmer could.

The oldies have grown very fond of Buttercup. Most of them treat her as if she is an overgrown dog, but she doesn't seem to mind.

'If you ever need a good home for her, she would be very welcome here,' the matron tells Dad.

'Oh no,' he says. 'We are trying to be self-sufficient, you see. When Buttercup is old enough, she will give us milk and cheese!'

'Pigs might fly,' one of the old ladies giggles. Pigs? I think she is getting her animals mixed up a little bit.

'Doris!' the matron says. 'That's not very nice! Whatever do you mean?'

'I mean there will be no milk or cheese,' Doris smirks, leaning on her Zimmer frame. 'I used to keep goats during the war, and I can tell you now that Buttercup is a billy goat. To put it bluntly, she is a HE.'

Dad's shoulders sag, and shortly afterwards Buttercup the billy goat moves into new, high-security quarters in the grounds of the Twilight Years Rest Home.

'How about fresh, free-range eggs for the residents too?' Dad says, as he settles Buttercup into his new quarters. 'One goat and three hens – I can't separate them.'

So Attila, Cleopatra and Esmerelda move in too, and Pixie and I visit them every day on our way home from school. I worry that there will be no eggs, because I cannot really sneak into the grounds of the rest home every morning to hide my shop-bought ones, and I worry that the whole gang of them will escape and terrorize Stella Street.

I imagine the Twilight Years cook making a huge goat-and-chicken pie. It doesn't bear thinking about.

However, it seems that Beth's grandad and Bert from next door can build much better chicken runs than Dad can, because there are no more escapes. Nobody complains about the lack of eggs, and when a group of us from school go in one day after class to learn how to bake fairy cakes with some of the old ladies, the cook tells us that they are getting three eggs a day, every day, without fail.

It looks like Buttercup and the chickens are happy at last, and I am glad about that.

As for the Star of the Week award, Miss Moon gives it to Murphy for his quick thinking during the fashion show; his on-the-spot speech may not have made much sense, but  it made me look a lot less stupid. Well, a bit.

 The week after, Beth and Willow get the award jointly, for helping in the fashion-show rescue and being such supportive

friends; and the week after that Ethan Miller gets the award for making the table football game, which apparently is still a big hit with the oldies.

I cannot really complain, I suppose.

For once, I actually did something good. Beth is back to her usual chirpy self. Her grandad is happily growing cabbages and dahlias, just like he always did, only in the grounds of the Twilight Years Rest Home. Beth's gran comes out to flirt with him every day, which is very sweet considering she can't actually remember that they have been married for almost fifty years.

Besides, I get my moment of fame in the end. *The Evening News* finally do send a photographer down to the Twilight Years Rest Home, to do a double-page spread on its new links with Stella Street Primary. There is a nice picture of Dad and Bert digging the new veggie garden, a shot of Ethan playing table footy with the oldies and one of Beth, Willow and some of the old ladies knitting.

The biggest picture of all, though, is one of me – in pink wellies and a rainhat, with a chicken under each arm and mud smeared right across my nose.

Predictably, Buttercup is at my side, chewing a mouthful of my skirt.

It is not exactly the cover of *Vogue* magazine, but I am quite glad about that.

I can see now that I am not model material, not one little bit. I am more rolling around in the mud material.

Perhaps I would have fitted in on the Isle of Muck after all!

Pixie, Murphy and me buy the paper on the way home from school, scanning through the feature as we walk.

' "*Strong links have been forged between the pupils of Stella Street Primary and the Twilight Years Rest Home,*" '
Murphy reads aloud, biting into a custard doughnut.

' "*Shared football, reading, bingo, knitting and cookery groups now run weekly, and residents are enjoying the new Community Garden, pet chickens and goat . . .*" '

'Who knew so much would come of one little idea?' I say.

'Listen to this bit,' Murphy says. ' "*The project was the idea of Year Six student Daizy Star. Miss Moon, project co-ordinator and Year Six teacher, told our reporter: 'Daizy is full of good ideas and always keen to help others. She really is a model pupil.'*" '

Murphy and Pixie laugh so hard they just about choke on their doughnuts, but my cheeks flush pink at the compliment and I stand a little taller. I am a model pupil after all – it is almost better than getting a Star of the Week award.

All's well that ends well . . . isn't it?

We turn the corner into Silver Street and a strange, sickly smell hits us. This has happened before. I get a bad, bad feeling.

Dad wouldn't. He couldn't. Could he?

'It's not manure,' Pixie whispers. 'Is it?'

'Don't think so,' Murphy frowns. 'It smells more like . . . rancid chip fat!'

'It's getting stronger,' Pixie whimpers. 'I don't like it, Daizy!'

I don't like it, either. And I don't like the huge, rusting van parked up outside our house, engine shuddering, either. The bumper seems to be held on with string and parcel tape, and there is no doubt about it – the sickly, chippy stink is coming from the exhaust pipe.

The engine splutters and dies, and Dad gets down from the cab.

'So!' he beams. 'How do you like our new transport? It's lean, clean and totally green! It's a triumph of recycling. Can you believe it? The engine actually runs on old chip fat!'

'I can believe it,' I say, holding my nose. 'Dad, please tell me this heap of junk isn't our new car?'

'It is,' he says proudly. 'But it's much, much more than just a car, Daizy.'

There is a heavy, sinking feeling in my stomach, as if I have eaten one too many nettle flapjacks.

Dad grins.

'I've just had the most *amazing* idea . . .'

# It all started with a Scarecrow.

**Puffin is seventy years old.**
Sounds ancient, doesn't it? But Puffin has never been
so lively. We're always on the lookout for the next big
idea, which is how it began all those years ago.

Penguin Books was a big idea from the mind of
a man called Allen Lane, who in 1935 invented
the quality paperback and changed the world.
**And from great Penguins, great Puffins grew,
changing the face of children's books forever.**

The first four Puffin Picture Books were hatched in 1940 and the
first Puffin story book featured a man with broomstick arms called
Worzel Gummidge. In 1967 Kaye Webb, Puffin Editor, started the
Puffin Club, promising to **'make children into readers'**.
She kept that promise and over 200,000 children became
devoted Puffineers through their quarterly instalments of
*Puffin Post*, which is now back for a new generation.

Many years from now, we hope you'll look back and
remember Puffin with a smile. **No matter what your age
or what you're into, there's a Puffin for everyone.**
The possibilities are endless, but one thing is for sure:
whether it's a picture book or a paperback, a sticker book
or a hardback, **if it's got that little Puffin
on it – it's bound to be good.**